Penguin Readers

THE TALENTED MR. RIPLEY

PATRICIA HIGHSMITH

LEVEL
6

RETOLD BY ANNA TREWIN
ILLUSTRATED BY JULIA CASTAÑO
SERIES EDITOR: SORREL PITTS

Contains adult content, which could include: sexual behavior or exploitation, misuse of alcohol, smoking, illegal drugs, violence and dangerous behavior.

This book includes content that may be distressing to readers, including references to suicide, and abusive or discriminatory treatment of individuals, groups, religions or communities.

PENGUIN BOOKS

UK | USA | Canada | Ireland | Australia
India | New Zealand | South Africa

Penguin Books is part of the Penguin Random House group of companies
whose addresses can be found at global.penguinrandomhouse.com.
www.penguin.co.uk www.puffin.co.uk www.ladybird.co.uk

The Talented Mr. Ripley first published in 1955.
First published in Great Britain by The Cresset Press, 1956
This Penguin Readers edition published by Penguin Books Ltd, 2022
001

Original text written by Patricia Highsmith
Text for Penguin Readers edition adapted by Anna Trewin
Original first published in 1955. Copyright © 1993 by Diogenes Verlag AG Zurich. All rights reserved.
Text copyright © Penguin Books Ltd, 2022
Illustrated by Julia Castaño
Illustrations copyright © Penguin Books Ltd, 2022
Cover design and illustration copyright © Liam Relph/Michael Salu, 1999

The moral right of the original author has been asserted

Printed and bound in Great Britain by Clays Ltd, Elcograf S.p.A.

The authorized representative in the EEA is Penguin Random House Ireland,
Morrison Chambers, 32 Nassau Street, Dublin D02 YH68

A CIP catalogue record for this book is available from the British Library

ISBN: 978-0-241-54261-3

All correspondence to:
Penguin Books
Penguin Random House Children's
One Embassy Gardens, 8 Viaduct Gardens,
London SW11 7BW

Contents

Note about the story

Patricia Highsmith (1921–1995) was an American writer. She is most known for her five books about the clever **fraudster*** Tom Ripley. *The Talented Mr. Ripley* was also made into a famous movie.

The story of *The Talented Mr. Ripley* happens in the 1950s, when most people traveled by ship rather than plane. Tom Ripley travels from the United States to Italy to find Dickie Greenleaf (the name "Richard" is shortened to "Dickie") and bring him home to his father.

Before-reading questions

1 The story of *The Talented Mr. Ripley* happens in the 1950s. What do you know about life in the 1950s? How was it different from life now?

2 Much of the story happens in Italy. What do you know about Italy and its big cities? Have you ever visited any of them? If so, what were they like?

3 Have you ever wanted to live another person's life? If yes, whose life would you like to live?

4 How important is money in your life? What things would you do if you were very rich?

*Definitions of words in **bold** can be found in the glossary on pages 107–112.

CHAPTER ONE

Tom makes a promise

Tom looked behind him and saw the man coming out of the Green Cage bar, heading his way. Tom walked faster, but the man was definitely following him. He had first noticed him five minutes ago, watching him from a table as if he was not quite sure. But he had looked sure enough for Tom to pay for his drink and quickly leave.

Tom ran across Fifth Avenue. Should he go into Raoul's Bar and have another drink? Or should he try to escape the man down Park Avenue? He decided on Raoul's. He went in and ordered himself a **gin and tonic**. Then, he stood at the bar and watched the door.

A few minutes later, the man entered. Was he a policeman or a detective? He did not look like either. He looked like a businessman, somebody's father, well fed and gray-haired. My God, what did he want? "They couldn't give me more than ten years in prison, could they?" Tom thought.

The man came toward him, and Tom suddenly had a moment of terrible **regret**.

"Excuse me, are you Tom Ripley?" the man said.

"Yes."

"My name is Herbert Greenleaf. Richard Greenleaf's father." His face was friendly, smiling, and hopeful. "You're a friend of Richard's, aren't you?"

Tom started to remember. Dickie Greenleaf. A tall blond

man who Tom had known for a while. He had a lot of money.

"Oh, Dickie Greenleaf. Yes," he said.

"And you know Charles and Marta Schriever, don't you? They're the ones that told me about you, that you might—um, do you think we could sit down at a table?"

"Yes," said Tom, happily, and picked up his gin and tonic. He followed the man to an empty table. "I'm safe!" he thought. No one was going to arrest him. This was about something else. Maybe Richard needed help. Or maybe his father just needed advice. Tom knew what to say to a man like Mr. Greenleaf.

"I've seen you once before, I think," said the man, sitting down. "Didn't you come up to the house once with Richard?"

"I think I did."

"The Schrievers gave me a description of you." He turned to order a beer from the waiter. "We've all been trying to find you, then someone told them that you sometimes go to the Green Cage bar. The Schrievers seem to think you knew Richard quite well."

"I remember him, yes, but I don't think I've seen him for a couple of years."

"He's been in Europe for two years," said Mr. Greenleaf. "The Schrievers speak very highly of you and thought you might have some **influence** on Richard. I want him to come home. We need him here, but he won't listen to me or his mother. You see, I know so few of Richard's friends now."

Tom remembered going to a **cocktail** party at the Schrievers' with Dickie Greenleaf. So that's how it had happened. He had only met the Schrievers three or four times in his life—the last time was to help with Charley Schriever's tax bill and make it lower for him. Had Charley told Mr. Greenleaf that he was intelligent, honest, and happy to help people? That was a mistake.

"Why won't Richard come home?" asked Tom.

"He says he prefers living over there. But his mother's quite ill right now—she has **cancer** and may not live another year. He says he's painting, but he's not talented enough to be a painter. He could create beautiful boats though. You're the first of Richard's friends who has been happy to listen. They all think that I'm trying to control his life."

Tom could easily understand that. "I wish I could help," he said, politely. He remembered now that Dickie's money came from a shipbuilding company. Small sailing boats. His father must want him to come home and run the family business.

Tom was on the edge of his chair, about to stand up. But he could feel Mr. Greenleaf's disappointment. "Where's Dickie staying in Europe?" Tom asked, not caring where he was staying.

"In a village called Mongibello, south of Naples. Spends all his time sailing and painting. He's bought a house there. Richard has an **income** from a **trust fund**—nothing huge, but enough to live in Italy, he says. Are you working now?"

"I'm in the accounting department of a small company at the moment," Tom said.

Mr. Greenleaf watched him hungrily.

"How old is Dickie now?" Tom asked.

"He's twenty-five."

"So am I," thought Tom. Dickie was probably having a wonderful time in Italy. A trust fund, a house, a boat. Why should he want to come home? Dickie was lucky. What was he, Tom, doing at 25? Living from week to week. No bank account. Running away from the police now for the first time in his life. He was suddenly bored of the conversation with Mr. Greenleaf and wanted to be back at the bar by himself.

"I remember fishing with Dickie at a weekend party on Long Island," he said. "He was talking about going to Europe then. I'm sorry I'm not free or I'd be very happy to go over there and try to **influence** him into coming home."

"If you or somebody like you could get at least a couple

of months off from their job," said Mr. Greenleaf, "I'd be happy to pay for the **voyage** by sea and the living costs, in order to send them over to talk to him."

Tom's heart suddenly jumped in his chest, then he made himself look thoughtful. "I might be able to," he replied, carefully.

"Do you really think you might be able to arrange it? During this fall? I think Richard would listen to you."

It was already the middle of September. Tom stared at the thick gold ring on Mr. Greenleaf's little finger and smiled. "I think I might," he said. "I'd be glad to see Richard again—especially if you think I could help."

———

Mr. Greenleaf offered to take him home in a taxi, but Tom had not wanted him to see where he lived—in a dirty little apartment between Third and Second Avenue. He was staying with a man called Bob Delancey who he hardly knew, but who had offered him a room when he needed one. He had not invited any of his friends to Bob's place and had not told anyone where he was living. He was too **ashamed**. He knew he would not be living there for long, and now Mr. Greenleaf had **turned up**. Something *always* turned up, that's what Tom believed.

But there was one good thing about staying at Bob's place. He could get his George McAlpin post sent there without anyone finding out what he was really doing. He walked into his small bedroom and looked at the letters that had arrived addressed to a "George McAlpin" that morning. There was a **check** for $119, to be paid to the Collector of **Internal Revenue** from that lovely Mrs. Edith W. Superaugh. And paid without any complaining at all! This increased his total in checks to $1,863. He wished he could actually **cash** them. It was just a game really. He played it using some forms that he had stolen from the Department of Internal Revenue when he had worked for them for a short time. He was not stealing anything. But perhaps he should call just one more person before he sailed for Europe. He would tell them the same thing, that they owed extra tax to the Revenue, and see if they believed him. He was just waiting for one of the idiots to pay him in **cash**.

The next night, he went to dinner with the Greenleafs at their huge apartment on Park Avenue. Mr. Greenleaf welcomed him in a friendly voice that promised many drinks and a good dinner, and then he introduced Tom to his wife. "Emily, this is Tom Ripley!"

"I'm so happy to meet you!" she said, warmly. She was what he had expected—blond, tall, and slim—and very polite and nice. "I don't think we've met before. Are you from New York?"

"No, I'm from Boston," Tom said. That much was true.

Mr. Greenleaf led them into the dining room. They ate three **courses** that were brought to them by a **maid**, on a beautifully lit table. The dinner was wonderful and the conversation boring. They talked about Tom's job in "accounting," and his schooling. "Did you go to school in Boston?" asked Mr. Greenleaf.

"No, sir. I went to Princeton for a while." He hoped Mr. Greenleaf would ask him about Princeton, but he did not. Tom had been very friendly with a Princeton student and had gotten lots of information about the place from him. Tom told the Greenleafs some of the truth though—that he had been brought up by his Aunt Dottie in Boston. She had taken him to Denver when he was 16, and he had only finished high school there—he had not gone to Princeton or any other university. After he told them about his aunt, he felt uncomfortable, like he was in a movie, and suddenly someone would shout, "Cut!"

When they had finished the final course, Mrs. Greenleaf brought in some photos of Dickie in Europe. There was one of him in a café in what looked like Paris and another of him on a beach.

"This is Richard in Mongibello—on his boat," Mrs. Greenleaf said, pointing to a picture of Dickie in a boat next to a girl with curly blond hair who looked healthy, but not very **sophisticated**.

"And that's Marge Sherwood," Mrs. Greenleaf continued, "the only other American who lives there." Then, she looked down at the carpet.

"Mrs. Greenleaf," Tom said, gently. "I'm going to do everything I can to make Dickie come back."

CHAPTER TWO

Dickie and Marge

Tom hated water. He had never traveled anywhere on it before. His parents had **drowned** in Boston Harbor, and Tom had always thought this had something to do with it. For as long as he could remember, he had been afraid of water. It gave him a sick, empty feeling to think that in less than a week he would have water below him, miles deep, and he would have to look at it most of the time.

Tom had told Bob Delancey that he was leaving in a week, but Bob did not seem very interested. He decided not to tell any of his other friends that he was leaving. He wrote to his aunt in Boston explaining that he was going abroad and it might be months or even years before he came back. He asked her not to worry and not to send any more checks. He left her with no address so she would not be able to find him. It made him feel better—the checks were an **insult** when you considered how much money she might have sent him with her income.

She liked to tell him that looking after him had cost her much more than his father had left in insurance. Maybe it had, but did she have to keep telling him? He could also forget about the time she had sent him to get an ice cream while she sat in her car with her friend. When he came back, she kept driving away. "Come on! Come on, you slow thing," she had shouted. Then, she had turned and said to her friend, "He's a **sissy** through and through, just like his father."

On the morning of his sailing, Tom found a big basket of fruit in his **cabin** and a card that read: "*Bon voyage, Tom. All our good wishes go with you. Emily and Herbert Greenleaf.*"

Tom had never received a *bon voyage* basket before. To him, they had always been something that cost huge prices and were laughed at. Now, he found himself with **tears** in his eyes. He put his face down into his hands suddenly and began to cry.

———————

His **mood** on the voyage was calm and kindly, but he did not spend much time with other people. He wanted his time for thinking. But, when people sat at his table on the ship, he spoke to them pleasantly and smiled. He wanted to show himself as a serious young man with a serious job ahead of him. He had his own private income and was not long out of Princeton perhaps.

He was starting a new life. Goodbye to all the **second-rate** people he had spent time with during the last three years in New York. This was a fresh start. Whatever happened with Dickie, he would try his best and Mr. Greenleaf would know he had, and respect him for it.

———————

A week later, he was in France. He passed through Paris

quickly—he would come back here at some later time, he thought—and caught the sleeper train that would take him all the way to Rome. When he woke up the next morning, he was in Italy. He arrived in Naples late that afternoon and found a big hotel by the water. He had a difficult time ordering a fish dinner in a restaurant nearby because the waiter could not understand English. The next morning, he took a bus through Sorrento to the village of Mongibello. When it arrived, Tom jumped from the bus and pulled his suitcase down from the roof. There were houses above him on the mountain, and houses below, their roofs red against the blue sea.

He asked at the post office for Dickie's address, and an old man there tried to tell him in Italian, and show with his hands, where Dickie's house was. Tom then asked if he could leave his suitcase there, and the man seemed to understand. After asking a couple more people on the street, he finally came to a large house with two floors and a metal gate. Tom rang the bell outside the gate, and an Italian woman came out of the house.

"Mr. Greenleaf?" said Tom, hopefully.

The woman smiled and pointed down at the sea. Tom went into one of the little shops in the center of the village to buy some swimming shorts. But he could only find something black and yellow that was not much bigger than a **G-string**. He put it on, then walked down a narrow lane until he came to a beach where there were a couple of cafés and a restaurant with outside tables.

Tom walked along the beach until he saw him—about 300 feet away on the sand. His skin was burned dark brown from the sun, but it was definitely Dickie. He was with Marge.

"Dickie Greenleaf?" said Tom, who had taken off his shoes and was now walking quickly across the sand toward them.

Dickie looked up, but Tom could see that he did not recognize him. "Yes?"

"I'm Tom Ripley. I met you in the States several years ago. Remember? I think your father was going to write to you about me."

"Oh yes!" Dickie said. "This is Marge Sherwood. Marge, Tom—what was it?"

"Ripley."

"Nice to meet you," said Tom.

"Nice to meet you, too," replied Marge with a smile.

"How long are you here for?" Dickie asked.

"I don't know yet," Tom said. "I just got here. I'll have to look the place over."

Dickie was watching him with some **disapproval**, Tom felt. His arms were **folded**, his brown feet planted in the hot sand as he said, "I have to say, I don't really remember you from New York, but I can't remember much about America these days."

"Well, we're about to leave," said Marge, smiling. "Would you like to have lunch with us?"

"Yes, thank you. Thanks very much," replied Tom.

They made their way back up the hill, and fifteen minutes later Tom was sitting on Dickie's **terrace** with a gin and tonic in his hand. Marge was in the kitchen talking to the maid. Tom wondered if she lived here. The house was certainly big enough. It had Italian furniture, and there were two Picassos on the wall. They looked real.

Marge came out on to the terrace with her gin and tonic.

"That's my house over there." She pointed. "The square white one with the dark roof. I've been living there about a year."

She was wearing a red swimsuit with a shirt over it. She was not bad looking, and she had a nice body if you liked the solid type. Tom did not, himself.

Dickie came out with a cocktail. "How's my mother?" he asked.

"She seemed OK when I had dinner with your parents just before I left New York. I think your father was more worried a few weeks before. He's also worried because you won't come home."

"Herbert's always worried about something," said Dickie.

The maid brought out some food. Tom said nothing as Dickie and Marge discussed a restaurant in the village. He had nothing to offer the conversation so he sat looking at Dickie's thick gold rings. One had a green stone, and the other had a small picture cut into it.

"What hotel are you staying at?" Marge asked Tom, finally, and passed him a cup of coffee.

Tom smiled. "I haven't found one yet. Which one do you **suggest**?"

"The Miramare's the best. Giorgio's is cheap, but . . ."

"It's got insects in the beds that will bite you," finished Dickie.

"You're in a good mood today, aren't you?" Marge said, throwing a lettuce leaf at him.

"Then, I'll try the Miramare," Tom said, standing up.

"I must be going."

Neither of them encouraged him to stay. Dickie walked with him to the front gate while Marge stayed sitting down. Tom wondered if they were sleeping together. Marge was in love with Dickie, Tom decided, but Dickie did not care about her.

"I'd like to see some of your paintings sometime," Tom said to Dickie.

"Fine. Well I suppose we'll see you again if you're around."

"I enjoyed the lunch. Goodbye, Dickie."

"Goodbye."

The metal gate closed with a bang.

Tom took a room at the Miramare. He threw his suitcase on the floor, lay on the bed, and thought about Dickie. Why should he want to come back to subways and taxis and a nine-to-five job? It was not as fun as sitting on a beach all day and having long lunches, and owning his own house with a nice maid to look after him. Tom suddenly felt jealous. The letter from Mr. Greenleaf had probably put Dickie against him. He should have just sat next to him at a café and pretended it was a chance meeting. Tom was angry with himself for being so heavy-handed and without **humor** today. Nothing he took really seriously ever succeeded. He had found that out years ago.

"I'll let a few days go by," he decided. The first step was to make Dickie like him. He wanted that more than anything else in the world.

CHAPTER THREE
Tom makes a friend

Tom left it for three days. Then, he went to the beach on the fourth morning, close to noon. He found Dickie alone, reading an Italian newspaper in the same place he had seen him first, in front of some gray rocks.

"Good morning!" Tom called. "Where's Marge?"

"Good morning. She's writing a book so she's probably working a little late. She'll be down."

Dickie pulled on the Italian cigarette in the corner of his mouth. "So, what have you been doing? I thought you'd gone."

"Sick," said Tom, dropping his towel on the sand but not too near to Dickie's. "But I'm all right now."

He went into the water, not too far, and dropped down until it reached his shoulders. Then, he came slowly back to the beach.

"Can I invite you for a drink at the hotel before you go up to your house?" Tom asked Dickie. "And Marge, too, if she comes down. I have some gifts for you from your parents."

"Oh yes, thanks very much." Dickie went back to his newspaper. Tom lay down on his towel. Soon, they heard the church bell announce one o'clock.

"Doesn't look as if Marge is coming down," Dickie said. "Shall we go?"

Tom got up. They walked up to the Miramare, saying very little to each other. When they reached Tom's room, he gave Dickie some shirts and expensive socks that Mrs. Greenleaf had asked Tom to bring for her.

Now Dickie had the presents, Tom thought, he was probably going to refuse the invitation for a drink. Tom followed him to the door. "Your father's very worried about you staying out here, you know. He asked me to talk to you about it, which of course I won't. But I still have to tell him something. I promised to write to him."

"I'm happier here," Dickie replied. "I may go back for a few days this winter, but I can't work for him. How would I paint? I like painting, and it's my decision how I spend my life. So, thanks for the message and the clothes. It was very nice of you." Dickie held out his hand.

Tom could not take it. He was about to fail in Mr. Greenleaf's eyes. "I ought to tell you something else," Tom said with a smile. "Your father sent me over here to ask you to come home."

It was his last chance to make Dickie like him.

"What do you mean?" asked Dickie, **frowning**. "You're saying he paid for you?"

"I have six hundred dollars with me that he gave me for the trip," Tom replied, smiling. "He approached me in a bar in New York. He recognized me from one meeting at your house, and we both know the Schrievers, who said that I might be able to help him. I hardly know the Schrievers! I told him I wasn't a close friend of yours, but he felt sure

I could help if I came over. I told him I'd try."

He suddenly remembered Dickie's smile, the way the lips turned up at the ends. It was coming now.

"I'm sorry," said Tom. "I don't want you to think that I'm just using your father. I expect to find a job somewhere in Europe soon, and I'll pay him back the money."

"Oh, don't worry about it! He'll be taking it from the business."

They had a drink in the hotel bar, and then Dickie invited him to lunch at his house. Marge met them there, and they sat and drank gin and tonics like the first time, but now the **atmosphere** had completely changed. Dickie made Tom tell Marge what he was really doing in Italy, so he made the story really funny, and she laughed like it was the best thing she had heard in years.

"So, what kind of work do you do?" said Dickie. "You said you might get a job in Europe?"

"Oh, I can do lots of things. Cleaning cars, accounting. I'm very good with numbers. I can **forge** a **signature**, fly a helicopter, cook, and do a one-man show. Shall I show you?"

He jumped to his feet. "In the show, I'm an English woman in the American subway. She wants some American experiences." He began to act. The woman tried to buy a ticket, then she did a silly walk to the train, but got lost. Dickie fell back in his chair laughing, but Marge looked blank. "She looks like she doesn't have that kind of humor," Tom thought.

Tom drank some of his gin and tonic and felt pleased with himself. "I'll do another for you sometime," he said.

"Come on, Tom," said Dickie, standing up. "I'll show you some of my paintings."

Dickie led the way into a large room that had an **easel** in the middle of the floor. "This is one I'm working on of Marge right now." He pointed to the picture on the easel.

"Oh," said Tom. It was not good in his opinion, probably in anyone's opinion. Her wide smile wasn't right, and her skin was too red. Dickie showed him other pictures of the village and mountains, seas, and beaches. They were all boringly similar, with the same reds for the houses and blues for the seas. Mr. Greenleaf had been right about his son's painting. Yet it gave Dickie something to do, Tom supposed. He felt disappointed about this because he wanted Dickie to be so much more.

Dickie showed him around the rest of the house, and Tom could not see any signs of Marge in the bedroom. He was surprised to see so many books there though, because he had not thought of Dickie as clever, but perhaps he was wrong. But he did not think he was wrong in feeling that Dickie was bored at the moment and needed someone to show him how to have fun.

They drank a lot of wine with the lunch, but Marge being there stopped Tom from talking about the things that he would like to have talked about. After lunch, she went into the kitchen to make them coffee.

"How long are you going to be here?" Dickie asked.

"Oh, at least a week, I'd say," Tom replied.

"Because – " Dickie's face was a little red from the wine. It had put him in a good mood. "If you're going to stay here a little longer, why don't you stay with me? Unless you'd prefer to stay in a hotel, of course."

"I'd like that. Thank you very much," Tom said.

The next morning, he moved in.

CHAPTER FOUR
The kiss

Later the same day, Tom and Dickie went to Naples by bus, and then they traveled on to Rome in the evening. They met several friends of Dickie's in Naples including a loud red-haired American man called Freddie Miles, who Tom did not like. In Rome, they went to a music-hall show then got very drunk together, walking down streets laughing with their arms round each other's shoulders. They slept in a park, where they were woken by the police in the early hours of the morning.

Following that, they traveled home and slept until four, when they were woken by Marge. She was obviously angry because Dickie had not sent her a **telegram** to let her know that he was spending the night in Rome.

"Not that I mind, but I thought that you were in Naples, and *anything* can happen in Naples," she told them.

She was looking at them both strangely. Tom kept his mouth shut. He had decided to let what they had done together be a mystery. She had a look of disapproval that a mother or an older sister might wear. Or was she jealous perhaps? She seemed to know that the two of them had become better friends in the last twenty-four hours than Dickie ever could be with her, just because Tom was another man. That was whether Dickie loved her or not, and Tom was sure that he did not.

But after a few minutes the anger left her face. Dickie went out of the room, and Tom asked her about the book she was writing. It was about Mongibello, she said, and she was going to put her own photographs in it. Tom hated her high voice and the way she said things, but he tried to be nice to her, because he could afford to be. He walked with her to the gate, and they said a friendly goodbye, but neither mentioned seeing each other later or tomorrow. She was definitely a bit angry with Dickie.

———————

For three or four days, Tom and Dickie saw very little of Marge except down at the beach, and she was certainly cooler toward both of them. Tom could see that Dickie was a bit worried, but not enough to talk to her about it because he had not seen her alone since Tom moved in. Tom had been with Dickie every moment.

Dickie seemed to love Tom's humor. He had lots of funny stories about people he knew in New York, some of them true, some of them not. They went sailing in Dickie's boat every day, and they never talked about when Tom was leaving.

Tom wrote a letter to Mr. Greenleaf:

> . . . *I think that Richard is thinking about whether to spend another winter here. I shall do everything I can to stop him from being here for another Christmas. In time, I may be able to get him to move back to the States . . .*

Tom smiled as he wrote it because it was all lies. He and Dickie were already talking about going to Paris. Then, they planned to go sailing around the Greek islands this winter and then skiing in Cortina, although Tom had never skied. They even talked about spending January and February in Majorca. And Marge would not be going with them, Tom was sure.

November came, and Tom was working hard to learn Italian, which pleased Dickie, who had even found a 23-year-old Italian boy called Fausto to give Tom lessons. They continued to see little of Marge, though one lunchtime Tom said to Dickie that he was worried they were not including her enough. He even suggested leaving Mongibello so that he did not come between them. Dickie replied that was stupid, but that afternoon he went on his own to try to **make** it **up** with Marge, which disappointed Tom. A little later, Tom was walking up the steps to Marge's house—he was planning to apologize to her—when he saw them on the terrace together. Dickie's arm was round her, and he was giving her small kisses on her cheek and smiling at her.

Tom ran back down the steps, wanting to scream. He arrived back at the house, breathing hard, and went into Dickie's painting **studio**, his mind shocked and blank. That kiss—it had not looked like a first kiss.

He went up to Dickie's bedroom and walked around for a few moments. He wondered when Dickie was coming back. Or was he going to stay and make an afternoon of it, take Marge to bed with him? Tom pulled open the door of Dickie's wardrobe and looked in. There was a new-looking gray suit that he had never seen Dickie wearing. He took it out and, taking off his shorts, put on the trousers. Then, he put on a pair of Dickie's shoes and a clean blue-and-white shirt. They all fitted him well.

"Marge, you must understand that I don't *love* you," Tom said into the mirror in Dickie's voice. "Marge, stop it!" His hands held the air as if they were holding Marge's throat. He shook her, until she sank lower and lower. "You know why I had to do that! You were getting between Tom and me."

Then, he moved to the window and looked toward Marge's house. Dickie was not on the steps or any part of the road that he could see. Maybe they were having sex. He imagined it, difficult and uncomfortable for Dickie, and Marge loving it. He took one of Dickie's hats and put it on his head. It surprised him how much he looked like Dickie in the mirror. His nose, the lower part of his face. It was only his darker hair that was very different from Dickie's.

"What are you *doing?*"

Tom turned round. Dickie was at the door.

"Oh, just having fun," Tom replied in the deep voice he always used when he was ashamed. "Sorry, Dickie."

Dickie **slammed** the door behind him. "Get out of my clothes," he said.

Tom started undressing, his fingers moving slowly and heavily because of his shock. Until now, Dickie had always said "wear this" and "wear that" about his clothes. He knew that Dickie would never say it again.

"Did you make it up with Marge?" Tom asked.

"Marge and I are fine," Dickie replied, in a way that shut Tom out from the two of them. "And another thing I want to say," he said, looking at Tom, "I'm not **gay**. I don't know if you think I am or not."

"Gay?" Tom smiled, but only a little. "I never thought you were gay."

"Well, Marge thinks *you* are."

Tom felt the blood go from his face. He kicked off a shoe. "Why?" he said. "Why should she? What've I ever done?" No one had ever said it directly to him before. Not in this way.

"It's just the way you behave," Dickie said in a **disapproving** way, then slowly opened the door. He walked out of the room without saying more.

Tom put his shorts back on and hurried downstairs to find Dickie making himself a drink.

"Dickie, it's important for you to know that I'm not gay, and I don't want anyone thinking I am."

"All right," Dickie said in a low, cross voice.

Tom's mind went back to certain groups of people he had known in New York. Known and then finally dropped. He **regretted** now having ever known them. When a couple of the men had tried to kiss him, he had rejected them. However, later he had bought them drinks or taken them to their homes in taxis because he did not want them to dislike him. He remembered, too, his aunt calling him a "sissy," and how ashamed he had felt when one friend had said, "Oh, **for God's sake**, Tommie, shut up!" And just because he had said in front of a group of people, "I can't decide if I like men or women, so I'm thinking of giving them *both* up."

Actually, he was one of the most clean-minded people he knew. That was what was so crazy about this situation with Dickie.

"I feel as if I've—" Tom began, but Dickie was not even listening. He turned away and carried his drink to the corner of the terrace.

"Are you in love with Marge, Dickie?"

"No," Dickie replied. "But I feel sorry for her. I care about her, and she's been very nice to me. We've had some good times together. You don't seem to understand that."

"I do understand. I thought that you only cared for her as a friend, but that she was in love with you."

"She is. You try not to hurt people who are in love with you, you know. I haven't been to bed with her, and I don't plan to. But I want to keep her as a friend."

"Of course."

Tom decided to give Dickie some space and went into the village for a coffee. He was glad that Dickie was not angry with him any more, that he was not planning to tell him to leave. Tom knew Dickie's moods. By five o'clock, after he had finished painting, everything would be forgotten, Tom was sure. Dickie would be back to normal.

CHAPTER FIVE

A change of plan

Tom walked quickly into the studio where Dickie was painting.

"Want to go to Paris in a **coffin**?" he asked.

"What?" said Dickie, looking up from his picture.

"I've been talking to an Italian man in Giorgio's. We'd get a hundred thousand **lire** each. I think it's a way of getting **drugs** there. He said there would be three coffins and there would be a real dead person in the third coffin. They would put drugs inside that person. We would get the trip, the money, and the experience. What do you think?"

There was a strange smile on Dickie's face, as if he thought Tom was joking.

"I'm serious," said Tom.

Then, Dickie's look changed. "Are you sure this man hadn't taken drugs himself? He's probably just a dirty **crook**. If you want to do it then go ahead, but I don't."

Tom suddenly felt anger rise in his blood. "In October, when we went to Rome, you would have thought this thing was fun," he said.

"Oh, I don't think so," replied Dickie, angrily.

Tom suddenly wanted to leave Dickie. He did not like the **arrogant** way he said "crook," like Dickie was above the other man just because he was **wealthy**. But then Tom's anger suddenly left him.

He wanted to make it up but did not know what to say. Dickie stared back at him with eyes that were empty and cold, and Tom suddenly felt an awful pain in his chest. They were not friends, they did not know each other, and it was the same for every person he had known and would ever know. He had failed.

"I think I'm going to go and see Marge for a while," Dickie said, flatly, and walked out.

After Dickie had left, Tom went to the post office to get his post. There was a letter from Mr. Greenleaf.

My dear Tom,

As you have been with Dickie for over a month and he shows no signs of coming home, I can see you haven't been successful. I want you to know that my wife and I send our thanks for trying so hard, but we feel it is time to stop now. I hope that you have enjoyed the trip to Italy despite everything.

With thanks,
  H. R. Greenleaf

Tom walked slowly back up the hill. It was the end of the story, he knew it. He imagined Dickie and Marge's conversation. Tom knew what Marge would say: "Why don't you just *tell him to go?*"

When Dickie came home, Tom did not show him his father's letter. Instead, he said, "Do you think Marge would come up to Paris with us, when we go?"

Dickie looked surprised. "I think she would."

"Well, ask her," Tom said, cheerfully.

"But I don't know if I should go up to Paris," Dickie said, slowly. "I'd like to get away for a few days, but Paris . . ." He lit a cigarette. "I'd be just as happy to go up to San Remo. It's a lot closer."

"But when *will* we go to Paris?"

"I don't know. Any time. You go there if you want."

Tom listened to Dickie's **tone**. He felt sure that Mr. Greenleaf had told Dickie that he was tired of Tom and thought he was just using his money to have a good time. Only the other day, Dickie had asked Tom if he was going home for Christmas, knowing that he did not have a home to go to. It had been a **hint** that he should leave, he knew it.

"Well—I suppose we'll go to San Remo instead then," Tom said, but inside he could have cried and his hands were shaking.

"All right," said Dickie.

———

Marge did not want to come with them to San Remo. She was having a good "run" on her book.

"But please can you try to find me that **perfume**, Dickie," she said. "You know, the Stradivari one I couldn't find in Naples."

They took only one suitcase of Dickie's with them, because they only planned to be away for three nights and four days. Dickie was a bit happier now, but the awful feeling that this would be their final trip together was still there. Tom had never felt like a boring guest before, but this was how Dickie made him feel now. He stared at Dickie's rings and listened to him chat on about how small San Remo was and how he had spent a week there once with Freddie Miles. Then, as the train was coming into the town, he suddenly said, "By the way, Tom, I hope you don't mind terribly, but I think I'd like to go to Cortina with Marge this winter, you know, alone. You can't ski anyway, can you?"

Tom's body immediately went stiff, but he tried not to show it.

"Of course," he said, then nervously looked at the map he was holding. But Dickie was already pulling their suitcase down.

"We're not far from Nice, are we?" Tom asked.

"No."

"And Cannes. I'd like to see Cannes. At least it's in France."

"Well, let's go then. You brought your passport, didn't you?"

Tom had brought his passport, so they took a train and arrived there at eleven that night. Tom thought Cannes was beautiful with its long line of expensive hotels looking out over the water. Dickie chose a smaller hotel on a back street—the Gray d'Albion. It was nice enough, but if Tom had chosen he would have gone to one on the seafront.

They had breakfast at a café the next morning, then walked down to the sea. It was cool, but not too cool for swimming. The beach was almost empty except for a group of men in yellow G-strings who were playing some kind of strange game. As he and Dickie came closer, Tom could see that they were **acrobats**.

"Look!" cried Tom. "They're building a human tower."

He and Dickie watched as the men climbed on each other's shoulders. When the last one—a boy of about 17—reached the top and put his arms in the air, Tom clapped his hands together. "Well done!" he shouted, and the boy smiled and waved back at him.

Then, Tom turned and saw the strange look that Dickie was giving him. He clearly thought the acrobats were gay. Maybe Cannes was full of gay people, but so what? Tom realized his body was stiff with anger.

Dickie stood with his arms folded. "Are you going to swim?" Tom asked.

"I don't think so," Dickie said. "Why don't you stay here and watch the acrobats in their G-strings? I'm going back." Then, he turned and started walking toward the hotel before Tom could answer.

They left for San Remo that afternoon, and Dickie let Tom pay the hotel bill. Tom had also bought their train tickets, although Dickie had just cashed one of his trust-fund checks and had plenty of money with him.

On the train, Dickie rested back his head and closed his eyes, saying nothing. Tom stared at his arrogant, handsome face and was filled with a mix of crazy **emotions**. He felt **insulted** and wanted to kill Dickie. It was not the first time he had thought of it. The idea had come to him two or three times before and had lasted just a second or two, before leaving him ashamed. But now he thought about it for a full two minutes, because he was leaving Dickie anyway, and why should he be ashamed any more? He hated Dickie. He had wanted to be his friend, but Dickie had rejected him. He was pushing Tom out into the cold.

If he killed Dickie on this trip, Tom thought, he could just say that an accident had happened. Then, suddenly, a brilliant idea came to Tom. He could become Dickie Greenleaf himself! They looked so much like each other—he even fitted Dickie's clothes. He would not be able to live in a place where Dickie had actually known people of course. And his hair was a bit darker than Dickie's, but he could make it lighter. Then, he could use Dickie's passport and do everything that Dickie did. He could go and get Dickie's things from Mongibello, tell Marge a stupid story, and then get an apartment in Rome or Paris. He could receive Dickie's check every month and forge his signature.

The danger of it suddenly made Tom feel excited. And then, slowly, he began to think of *how*.

CHAPTER SIX

In San Remo

They arrived in San Remo, which was another small town with shops and hotels on the seafront. Tom thought about where and how he would kill Dickie. In the streets at night, perhaps. They would be dark and silent by one in the morning, if he could keep Dickie awake that long. But how would he **get rid of** the body? It had to completely disappear. That left only the water, but Dickie was a strong swimmer while Tom was not.

There were little blue-and-white **motorboats**, Tom noticed, that people could rent at the beach from an Italian man. In each motorboat was a heavy **anchor**.

"How about we rent a boat, Dickie?" Tom asked, excitedly.

Dickie looked at him strangely because Tom had not been excited about anything since they had arrived here. Then, he looked out to sea. It was ten thirty in the morning, and the sky was gray, the kind of November gray that would not disappear all day.

"Well, all right," Dickie replied. "Just for an hour." Then, he immediately jumped into a boat and the Italian man started it for them. As Tom got in after Dickie, he noticed a single **oar** lying in the bottom of the boat. Dickie turned the boat and headed away from the town.

"This is great!" he said, his hair blowing in the wind, and Tom could see in his eyes that he was remembering other boat trips with Marge, or Freddie Miles perhaps. He sailed further and further away out into the empty sea. Tom smiled, but inside he was getting frightened. If something happened to the boat, there was no chance that he could get back to land. But neither was there a chance that anyone could see what they did here. He could hit Dickie, jump on him or kiss him, and no one would see.

Tom suddenly stood up and started taking off his clothes. "Shall I jump in?" he said. "I'll go in if you will."

"Will I? Sure!" Dickie slowed the **motor** so that the boat stopped moving forward and began taking off his shirt and his trousers.

"Come on then!" he said, noticing that Tom still had his trousers on.

At that moment, Tom picked up the oar and hit the top of Dickie's head with it.

"Hey!" Dickie shouted, and his body sank heavily to one side. His eyes were wide with confusion and surprise.

Tom brought down the oar again, harder this time.

"For God's sake!" Dickie said in a strange voice, before the oar hit him for a third time, and he fell heavily into the bottom of the boat. Tom hit him again and again, until Dickie's eyes closed and his body went still. The bottom of the boat was filled with Dickie's blood.

Then, Tom looked all around him. There was nothing on the water except for a small white motorboat some miles away, which was traveling fast toward the beach.

Tom immediately pulled off Dickie's rings and put them in his pocket. There were cigarettes, a **wallet**, and a pencil in Dickie's jacket, and three keys on a chain in his trouser pocket. Tom took them all. Then, he untied the anchor rope from the boat and instead tied it very tightly round Dickie's bare ankles. He thought the rope was about 35 or 40 feet long. "The weight should be just enough to hold the body under the water," he thought.

Tom threw the anchor over the side of the boat. The anchor went under the water with a *ker-plung* sound, and soon the rope round Dickie's ankles went tight. Tom lifted them over the side of the boat and started pulling at Dickie's arms. He tried to push the body into the water, but it was heavier than he thought, and the boat started rolling wildly from side to side. Finally, Dickie fell into the water but Tom lost his balance and fell backward against the motor, which made a sudden loud noise. The boat jumped forward, throwing Tom into the water, too.

The next moment, his head came up above the water; he was shouting and fighting for air. He did not want to drown after all this! He reached out for the side of the boat, but it was moving round him in crazy circles. Twice, three, four times, it came close to his hands as he caught one breath of air. He shouted for help. He got nothing but a mouthful of water. The boat came close again, and he tried with all his strength to reach it. This time his fingers just caught the side. He half pulled himself up on to the side of the boat and reached for the motor. The boat slowed, then stopped.

Tom stayed hanging on to the boat's side, resting and breathing hard. Slowly, he lifted one leg and the other, and pulled himself back in. His whole body ached, and he had blood on his hands from the boat. He checked his pockets to make sure he still had Dickie's rings. Then, he began to think about what to do with the boat. He had planned to return it, but it was impossible now. Blood, he knew, was very hard to get rid of.

He would have to hide the boat instead. He turned the motor back on, and headed slowly toward the land until a small beach came into view, with rocks and trees around it. There were no people there. He took the boat toward the beach until he felt it brush the sand under it. Then, he got out carefully and began to collect lots of stones, all about the size of a human head. He dropped them, one by one, into the boat. When he had enough stones, he walked with the boat out into the water as far as he could go, then pulled one side down again and again as hard as he could until water began to pour in. Slowly, the boat sank. Then, Tom walked through the water back to the beach. When he reached it, he fell on to his stomach and rested, face down, on the sand.

―――――――

He returned to Mongibello the next day, after getting the sleeper train to Naples. The man at the hotel desk in San Remo had asked where his friend was, and he had replied that they were meeting at the train station. No one else had asked any questions.

When he got off the bus, he immediately saw Marge. She was walking through the village on her way to the beach.

"Where's Dickie?" she asked.

"He's in a hotel in Rome." Tom smiled, easily. "He's staying up there for a few days. I came back to get some of his things for him. How's everything here?"

"Oh, boring," said Marge. She looked uncomfortable with him, but still she followed him up the hill and into Dickie's house. "You look like you've had a good time," she said, a bit sadly. "How long do you think Dickie's going to be away?"

"We did." Tom smiled. "I don't really know. He wants to see some art shows up there, and just be somewhere else for a bit." Tom made himself a large gin and tonic. Then, he reached for the suitcase. "Oh, and here's your Stradivari.

We got it in San Remo."

"Oh, thanks very much." Marge took the perfume and smiled.

"I'm going up to Rome tomorrow to join him," Tom said.

"Right, well, have a good time. And tell Dickie to write me a postcard. What hotel is he staying at?"

"It's one near the Piazza di Spagna."

"The Inghilterra?"

"That's it," Tom replied. "But I think he said to use the American Express for an address. I'll probably go down to the beach tomorrow morning before I leave."

"All right. Thanks for the perfume."

She walked down to the metal gate, and left.

CHAPTER SEVEN
A new start

Tom spent that evening collecting and packing Dickie's things. He took letters, keys, and some insurance documents. He took shirts, trousers and sweaters, drawing books, and notebooks. Then, he started looking around at the pictures and furniture. He would ask *Signor* Pucci, the manager of the Miramare, to manage the sale of the house and boat. Dickie had told him that Pucci did jobs like that for people in the village.

He had wanted to take all of Dickie's things immediately, but was worried about what Marge would think about him taking so much for such a short time. He decided it would be better to tell her that Dickie had now written saying that he wanted to move to Rome. To help this plan, he went to the post office the following afternoon and collected a letter for Dickie. As soon as he got home, he started packing Dickie's best paintings. Soon after, Marge appeared.

"Still here?" she asked, coming into Dickie's room.

"Yes, I had a letter today from Dickie. He's decided he's going to move to Rome." Tom stood up and smiled a little, as if it was a surprise to him, too.

"*Move* to Rome? For how long?"

"The rest of the winter, he said."

"He's not coming back all winter?" Marge's voice sounded lost.

"No. He might even sell the house. He said he was going to write to you. He said of course he can't go skiing with you now, but you should still go. I have the feeling he wants to be alone."

She was shocked and silent. Her face looked very upset, and she had tears in her eyes. After a minute, she said, "Are you going to stay with him in Rome?"

"Maybe for a while, to help him move in somewhere. I want to go to Paris this month, then I'll probably leave for America in the middle of December."

Just wait until she got the letter he was going to send her from Rome, Tom thought. He would be gentle with her, but he would make her feel sure that Dickie did not want to see her again.

─────────

Tom wore a cap in the hotel in Rome and gave them Dickie's passport at the desk instead of his own. The receptionist only looked at it quickly and did not ask any questions. When he got to his room, he took out Dickie's old **typewriter** and wrote Marge a letter.

Dear Marge,

I've decided to take an apartment in Rome for the winter. Just wanted to get away from old Mongy for a while. I need to be by myself. Sorry I didn't say goodbye, but actually I'm not that far away and hope to see you now and then. I just didn't feel like collecting my things myself so I asked Tom to do it.

43

Maybe it will help if we don't see each other for a while. But going away will help me to discover how I really feel about you, so I'd prefer not to see you for a while, darling. I hope you understand. I may go up to Paris with Tom for a few days, unless I start painting immediately. I met an old painter named Di Massimo whose work I like very much. I'm going to paint with him in his studio.

Write to me at the American Express, Rome, until I have found an apartment. I'm sorry about Christmas, darling, but I don't think I should see you that soon. You can hate me or not for that.

All my love,
    Dickie

When Tom went out to post the letter, he went to a shop and bought some **make-up** that he thought he might need.

He spent the evening practicing forging Dickie's signature for the bank checks. Dickie's monthly check was going to arrive from America in ten days, and he had asked the bank to send it to the American Express in Rome. Then, he repeatedly imagined having conversations with Marge and Fausto and Freddie. Marge was the most likely to come to Rome, he thought. He spoke to her first as Dickie, as he imagined him speaking to her on the telephone, and then as Tom. He had to practice being Tom as well as Dickie, in case she found his hotel and came up to his room. If that happened, he would have to quickly take off the rings and change his clothes. But mostly he was Dickie, discussing things in serious tones with Freddie and Marge, then chatting and laughing with Fausto, and with strangers at a dinner party. He practiced speaking in both English and Italian.

Every moment he spent in Rome was a pleasure, whether alone in his room or looking at art, or walking the narrow streets while he looked for an apartment. It was impossible to ever be sad or bored, he thought, while he was Dickie Greenleaf.

They called him "*Signor* Greenleaf" at the American Express, when he went there for his post. Marge's first letter said:

Dickie,

Well, it was a bit of a surprise. I wonder why you made the decision so quickly. Tom was behaving very strangely, and I'll believe he's leaving for America when I see it. May I say that I don't like that guy? I think he's just using you and is a bad influence. OK, he may not be gay, but he isn't normal enough to have any kind of sex life, if you know what I mean. He's just a nothing. You behaved like you'd realized this about him in the last few weeks, but now you're with him again, and I don't know what to think about it. However, I'm not interested in Tom but in you . . .

She went on then to talk about Christmas and how much she would miss him. She ended by thanking him for the perfume, and sending him love. She told him to write.

45

He put Marge's letter back in the envelope. Then, he decided to write a letter to Mr. and Mrs. Greenleaf on Dickie's typewriter.

Dear Mother and Dad,

I'm in Rome looking for an apartment. Sorry I've been so bad about letters recently. I hope to do better with the quiet life I'm leading here. I felt I needed a change from Mongibello, so I may sell the house and the boat. I've met a wonderful painter here called Di Massimo who will teach me in his studio. I'm going to work really hard for a few months and see what happens.

Mother, I hope you haven't gone to great trouble for Christmas. I don't really need anything I can think of. How are you feeling? Can you get around much? How is Uncle Edward now?

With love,
   Dickie

Uncle Edward was a brother of Mrs. Greenleaf, who was ill in an Illinois hospital. Tom had learned this from the most recent letter to Dickie from his mother.

A few days later, Tom left for Paris by plane. No one questioned his passport because he had made his hair lighter. He made sure he frowned the same way as Dickie did in the photo. He took a room at the Hotel du Quai-Voltaire, which some Americans that he met in Rome had told him about. Then, he went out for a walk in the cold December evening. He walked with his head up and a smile on his face. He loved the sophisticated atmosphere of the city, which he had heard so much about. He bought a French newspaper and ordered a *fine à l'eau*—because Dickie had once said that this was his usual drink in France.

He smiled Dickie's smile at people. He was in Paris, and it was nearly Christmas! It was wonderful to sit in a café and to think of always being Dickie Greenleaf. By the next afternoon, he had been invited to a party by a French girl and an American man. He had started a conversation with them in a restaurant on the Boulevard Saint-Germain. There, he met lots of interesting, wealthy people and behaved like he had always wanted to behave at a party. This was the beginning of his new life. He got invited to more parties and met more wealthy people, but he did not go to any in case he met someone who knew Dickie. Then, he started traveling slowly back to Rome, stopping in Lyon and Arles, and moving on to Cannes, Nice, Monte Carlo. All the places he had heard of—and where he now felt that he belonged.

CHAPTER EIGHT

The visitor

There were two letters from Marge when he got back to Rome on January 4th. She was leaving her rented house on March 1st, she said. She had not yet finished her book, but was sending it with photographs to an American **publisher** who was interested in it. She wrote:

When am I going to see you? I hate missing a summer in Europe after another awful winter, but I think I'll go home early in March. I was thinking about coming up through Rome, and we could travel around a bit together to all the places we like. Is it possible? What do you think?

The second letter was shorter. Tom knew why. He had not even sent her a postcard from Paris. She said:

Have changed my mind. I've booked a boat to leave for America on February 28th. I'm sorry I'm not seeing you, but I realize now that you still don't want to see me. However, if you decide you want to make a trip down to Mongy before the 28th, you already know that you are welcome.

Marge

At first, Tom decided not to write back to her, but the thing that made him feel uncomfortable was that she might decide to try to find him in Rome. If she searched the hotels, she could find him, so he needed to find an apartment quickly. Then, he changed his mind and, on January 10th, wrote to Marge to let her know that he was back in Rome and that he was painting again with Di Massimo. He said that he missed her but wanted to wait a little longer before seeing her again. The letter was written with Dickie's lazy, arrogant voice, and really said nothing at all.

He then found himself an apartment in the Via Imperiale near the Pincian Gate. He did not plan to spend a lot of time in it—he just wanted a home somewhere, after years of not having one. And Rome was a cool place to live. How wonderful just to be able to say, "Yes, I keep an apartment in Rome!" As well as Marge's letter, he received one from *Signor* Pucci saying that he had sold three pieces of his furniture for 150,000 lire, and that he had a buyer for the boat. Tom was very happy about this and bought himself an expensive meal in a restaurant that night.

Tom spent most of this time quietly touring the city, buying nice things for his apartment and practicing being sophisticated Dickie Greenleaf. He was taking Italian lessons and thought that his Italian was now as good as Dickie's. He even knew the mistakes that Dickie had always made when speaking it—and Tom made sure that he made the same mistakes himself.

Tom opened a new bank account for Tom Ripley, and from time to time put some money into it. Dickie had two banks, one in Naples and one in New York, with about $5,000 in each. Tom opened the Ripley account with a couple of thousand and added the money from the Mongibello furniture. He had to remember that there were two people to take care of now.

Tom kept away from the Americans in Rome who might expect him to come to their parties. He was confident in everything he did and was sure that he would not make a mistake. From the moment he got out of bed, he was Dickie, brushing his teeth the way Dickie brushed his teeth, eating his morning eggs the way that Dickie ate them. He had even painted some pictures in the way that Dickie painted.

Marge still wrote to him. They were funny, sweet letters, which he hated. He did not even like touching them, and after he read them he always threw them in the rubbish. Finally, he wrote:

I'm giving up the idea of an apartment in Rome for the moment. Di Massimo is going to Sicily for several months and I may go with him. I wish you luck with Mongibello.

He had a ticket for Majorca by train to Naples and then the boat from Naples to Palma on the night of January 31st. He had bought two suitcases from Gucci—they were the best that he could find. He was in the middle of packing them one morning when his doorbell rang. Tom ignored it. It rang for a second time and still Tom ignored it. He continued packing, **folding** Dickie's shirts lovingly into the suitcases. He was doing this when there was a knock on the door. The doorman must have let them go up.

Tom's hands were hot, and he felt ill as he went to answer it. He opened the door a few inches.

"Hello!" the American voice said out of the darkness in the hall. "Dickie? It's Freddie."

Tom stepped back, holding the door open. "Dickie's just out to lunch. Otello's, I think. He should be back a little later."

Freddie Miles came in, looking around. How had he found the place, Tom wondered. Tom quickly took his rings off and put them in his pocket without Freddie seeing him do it.

"You're staying with Dickie?" Freddie asked, giving him a strange look.

"No, I'm just here for a few hours," Tom said. Now, he had to get rid of Freddie without the doorman calling, "*Buongiorno, Signor* Greenleaf!"

"I met you in Naples, didn't I?" Freddie went on. "Aren't you Tom? Marge told me Dickie had moved to Rome, but she didn't have any address except the American Express. It was lucky I found his apartment. I met someone at the Greco bar last night who knew his address. A young Italian man."

Tom wondered how this had happened because he had

not told *anyone* where he lived. Had the man followed him home one day or night? He imagined a young, hungry face following him in the dark. It made him feel ashamed.

Freddie looked down. "You have the same shoes that Dickie and I have. They're very well made, aren't they?"

They were Dickie's shoes. "Yes, they certainly are," Tom said. "Can I offer you a drink?"

But Freddie had walked toward the bedroom then stopped, looking at the suitcases on the bed. "Is Dickie leaving for somewhere, or did he just get here?" Freddie asked, turning.

"He's leaving. Didn't Marge tell you? He's going to Sicily for a while."

But suddenly Freddie's face had changed, he was staring at the silver bracelet Tom wore on his wrist. Freddie was looking at it as if he had seen it before.

"You *do* live here, don't you?" he said in a strange voice. "With Dickie, I mean. You're wearing his bracelet."

Tom could not think of anything to say. He could feel the **arrogance** and anger building in Freddie and was a little afraid of him. He was the kind of man who would hit someone if he thought they were gay.

"Otello's, you say? I'll try to find him. Nice to see you again," Freddie added, unpleasantly, then he turned and left the apartment.

A few moments later, Tom went to the door and opened it a little. He could hear Freddie talking in Italian downstairs. "Only *Signor* Greenleaf," the doorman was now saying to him. "No, *signor*, I do not think he has gone out today at all, but I could be wrong!" He laughed.

Tom immediately heard Freddie running back up the stairs. He stepped back into the apartment and closed the door. He knew that Freddie would not stop now until he had found Dickie.

Tom picked up a heavy glass **ashtray** as Freddie knocked for a second time. Then, he opened the door, and Freddie came into the room. "Listen, would you mind telling—"

The ashtray hit him between the eyes. For a moment, Freddie looked shocked and confused. Then, his legs bent under him, and he fell on to the floor. Tom kicked the door shut and hit Freddie with the ashtray again and again and again.

CHAPTER NINE
A bad dream

Tom listened at the door to see if he could hear the doorman's footsteps coming up the stairs. There was nothing—the man had not heard anything. It was only twelve forty—it was hours before it would get dark. He searched Freddie's pockets and found a wallet and some keys. There were two car keys on a ring that said FIAT. Inside the wallet was information about the car—a FIAT 1400, black, 1955. Tom looked out the window and there it was, parked opposite the apartment.

Tom sat and thought for a long time, and then, suddenly, he knew what he was going to do. He would make it look like the robbing of a drunk foreigner. He had lots of time, but he did not stop until the room was ready. He lit and burned down ten or so cigarettes, leaving them in the ashtrays. He put a half-full bottle of gin on the table and filled part of a large glass with it. Then, he poured some of it down Freddie's throat and drank some himself. He knew he would have to clean it all back up by the evening, because, in the story he was going to tell the police, Freddie left his house around seven. But the house needed to be untidy because he had to believe the story he was going to tell the police himself. And after he told it he would still be able to leave for Naples and Palma at ten thirty tomorrow morning.

He had not wanted to kill him at all. Freddie and his stupid ideas about Dickie being gay. Dickie was his good friend—of course he was not gay! Where was the sex? Where was the problem? He looked at the body and said, angrily, "Freddie Miles, you died because of your own dirty mind."

———

Soon after seven o'clock, he checked to make sure the doorman was not there and then put Freddie's arm over his shoulder and lifted him down the stairs. He was very heavy, but Tom had to get him outside and into the car. Tom was a bit drunk from a mixture of gin and wine— because if other people saw him *they* needed to think he was drunk. But the street was quite quiet. Tom opened the car door and pushed Freddie into it. Then, he put on a pair of gloves, wiped the door clean, and got into the driver's seat. He started the car and drove away down the hill and through the city until he reached a large **graveyard** on the Via Appia Antica. He stopped the car and, with some difficulty, pulled the heavy body out of it, leaving it behind a large tree. Then, he got back into the car and turned it toward Rome again. A few minutes later, he pulled the car into the side of the road and took the money out of Freddie's wallet before dropping it into a rubbish bin on the way.

At nine o'clock the next morning, the telephone rang. "*Signor* Greenleaf?" asked an Italian voice.

"*Sì.*"

The voice told him that the body of Frederick Miles had been found in a graveyard on the Via Appia Antica and that *Signor* Miles had visited him the day before. Was that right?

"Yes, that is right," said Tom.

"What time exactly?" asked the policeman.

"From noon until—maybe five or six in the evening. I'm not sure."

"Would you be able to answer some questions? No, you don't need to come to the police station . . . We will come to you at ten thirty. You must not leave the apartment before then."

Tom angrily put the phone down. He would miss his train *and* his boat now. All he wanted was to leave his apartment and get out of Rome.

———

Two policemen came. A short, older man with a polite, kind smile—he looked neither intelligent nor stupid—and a younger one.

"How was Freddie killed?" Tom asked.

"He was hit on the head and the neck with something heavy," the younger policeman replied. "And robbed. We think he was drunk. Was he drunk when he left your apartment yesterday?"

"We were both a bit drunk. Wine and gin," Tom said. He spoke in Dickie's Italian, making the same mistakes that

Dickie had always made. The policeman wrote it down and also the time that Tom said Freddie had been there—from

about twelve to six. He told them that Freddie had not said where he was going when he left. They asked him more questions—how friendly was he with Freddie, was Freddie alone, how drunk had he been? "Not so drunk that he couldn't drive," Tom told them.

"And what did you do yesterday after *Signor* Miles left?" the older policeman asked.

"I stayed here," Tom said. "After Freddie left I had a little sleep, and then I went for a walk about eight o'clock." He told them this because a man that he knew from the apartments had seen him come in at about quarter to nine. He also told them that he wanted to go to Majorca the next day.

"We need you to stay in the city for the next couple of days," the taller one told him. "I'm sorry if you have made travel plans. Good day, *Signor* Greenleaf."

———

Tom knew that the name Dickie Greenleaf and the address of his apartment would appear in all the papers the next day, so he decided to go and stay in a hotel. He did not want any more people calling for him at the apartment. He booked a room at the Albergo Inghilterra and then rang the police station to tell them where he would be staying. He was at the Inghilterra within an hour.

He went out in the evening to buy the newspapers, then went to a bar to sit and read them. They all reported on

Freddie's death:

AMERICAN MURDERED ON THE VIA APPIA ANTICA ...
VIA APPIA MURDER OF AMERICANO LAST NIGHT

Tom read every word. Every newspaper carried the name Richard Greenleaf and gave his address. They all said that Freddie had had a few drinks. Then, on the last page of the last newspaper he read:

BARCA AFFONDATA CON MACCHIE DI SANGUE TROVATA NELL'ACQUA POCO FONDO VICINO SAN REMO

He read it quickly, with more fear in his heart than when he had carried Freddie's body down the stairs. The boat had been found—and it immediately brought back that morning to him. Dickie sitting by the motor, Dickie smiling at him, Dickie's body sinking through the water. The newspaper said that blood had been found on the boat. The boat owner could probably tell the police the very day the boat had been lost and that it was two Americans who had taken it out and not returned it. The police could then check the hotels for that day and the name Richard Greenleaf would stand out like a red flag.

Tom's mind began working very fast. If they found Dickie's body, they would think it was *Tom's*. Then, it would be Tom Ripley who was murdered that day. They would think that Dickie had killed him, and Freddie, too!

When he got back to the hotel there was a message from Marge. She had called from Mongibello at three thirty-five and would call again. He told the receptionist that if she called again he would accept the call. He just had to keep on going and saying the right things to everybody. After that, he could go to Greece, or even India or Sri Lanka. Some place far away where no friend of Dickie's could find him. What a fool he was to think that he could stay in Rome!

He went up to his room and wrote a letter from Dickie to his parents. Then, Marge rang, and he spoke to her as Tom. He told her that Dickie had gone out to the police station but would be back soon.

"How is Dickie?" she asked. "Why does he have to talk to the police?"

"Oh, just because he had some drinks with Freddie that day. I've been up north. When I heard about Freddie, I came down to Rome to see Dickie. If it hadn't been for the police, I'd never have found him. Anyway, I'll tell him to ring you as soon as he's back, shall I?"

He put down the phone and lay on his bed. As he fell asleep, he thought of Dickie on the beach in Mongibello, his deep happy laugh. He was standing over him, water running from his hair, saying, "Tom! Wake up! I swam!" Suddenly, Tom pushed himself up in the bed, looking for Dickie, who seemed to be in every dark corner of the room. Tom moved quickly to the window and opened it, angry with himself because, for a moment, he had lost control of his mind.

CHAPTER TEN
In Sicily

The next morning, two police officers came to see him at the hotel. It was the same older officer as yesterday—his name was Roverini—with a different younger one.

"*Buongiorno*," Tom said. "Have you found anything new?"

"No," replied Roverini. "But another matter has come up. You are a friend of the American Tom Ripley?"

"Yes," Tom said. "But he went back to America a month ago."

"I see," replied the policeman. "We think he might be dead. You were with him in San Remo in November, weren't you?"

They had checked the hotels. "Yes."

"When did you last see him? In San Remo?"

"No, I saw him in Rome." Tom remembered that Marge knew he had gone back to Rome after Mongibello, because he had said he was going to help Dickie. "I don't know exactly when it was. I think I had a postcard from him from Genoa—he said he was going back to America. Why do you think he is dead?"

Roverini looked at his papers and then back at Tom. "Did you take a boat trip with Tom Ripley in San Remo? A little boat?"

"Yes, I think we did. Why?"

"Because a little boat has been found with blood in it.

It was lost on November twenty-fifth. That was the day you were in San Remo with Tom Ripley. Did you bring the boat back?"

"Of course."

"Do you still have the postcard that Mr. Ripley sent you?" asked Roverini.

"No, I don't." Tom ran his fingers worriedly through his hair in the way that Dickie sometimes did. "Why don't you try Paris? Or Genoa? He always stays in small hotels because he prefers them."

"Do you know any friends of Tom Ripley?"

Tom shook his head. "No. I don't even know him that well. I think he had a friend in Florence, but I don't remember their name."

"Well, we shall ask," said the second policeman.

"Before you go," Tom said, nervously, "I want to ask when I can leave the city. I was planning to go to Sicily. I would very much like to leave today if it is possible. I will be staying in the Hotel Palma in Palermo so it will be easy for you to reach me."

"Palermo," Roverini repeated. "Yes, I think that will be possible."

"Thank you," said Tom. "If you find out where Tom Ripley is, please would you let me know."

———

No police came for him at the Hotel Palma in the next few days, and there were no messages.

He relaxed and began to enjoy Palermo. He loved the large square and the beautiful old buildings. He enjoyed spending the evenings alone, looking at Dickie's things—his rings on his own fingers, or his wallet and shirts. After Sicily, would come Greece—he definitely wanted to see Greece. He wanted to see it as Dickie Greenleaf with Dickie Greenleaf's money. But would things keep stopping him? He had not wanted to murder anyone, it had just been necessary. He really did not want to go to Greece as Tom Ripley, an ordinary tourist. He wanted to cry when he thought about that.

A letter came for him the next morning from Marge. He was glad when he read it.

Why didn't you call me back from the hotel? Or did Tom not tell you that I had rung? It is obvious now that you are running away from me. Why can't you tell me that you can't live without your little friend? I'm just sorry that you weren't brave enough to tell me that you are gay. I think you should know that I've told the police that Tom Ripley is with you—they seem desperate to find him (why, what has he done now?).

I've changed my boat and am leaving for America at the end of March. I expect we'll never see each other again. No hard feelings, Dickie. I just thought you were braver than that. Thank you for all the wonderful times we spent together. Best wishes for the future.

Marge

Later that day, Tom wrote another letter to the Greenleaf family on Dickie's typewriter. He told them about Freddie Miles and said that the police had finished their questioning. He told Dickie's mother about his health, which was good, and asked about hers although he did not use the word cancer.

Five days passed. Calm, quiet, pleasant February days spent wandering about Palermo. But Tom was sad. He wanted a group of bright new friends, but now he realized that could not happen. Not unless he went to somewhere like Istanbul or Sri Lanka, and what use were the second-rate kind of people he would get to know there? But there was always Capri. That was still Italy. He had wanted to go there before, but Dickie had decided against the idea.

On February 12th—the sixth day—a letter came for him from Dickie's bank in Naples. They asked him about the signature on the January receipt for his trust money, which they **suspected** had been forged.

Tom's blood turned cold. He decided to write to the bank to say that no money was **missing**, but how long would that keep them away? He had signed three receipts for Dickie's money beginning in December. Would they realize that all three signatures had been forged?

Two days later, he received another letter, this time from the police, asking him to return urgently to Rome to answer some important questions about Tom Ripley.

CHAPTER ELEVEN
In Venice

Tom quickly destroyed the letter from the police and began to pack quickly. He needed to get rid of all Dickie's things, but how and where? Should he throw them off the boat on the way to Naples? Suddenly, he knew what he had to do after leaving Sicily. He would not go anywhere near Rome. He would buy an old car that had done lots of miles. He would say he was traveling around Italy for the last two or three months. He had not known that the police were looking for him.

He went on packing. This was the end of Dickie Greenleaf, he knew. He hated becoming Thomas Ripley again, hated being nobody. He hated putting on his old clothes and feeling that people looked down on him and were bored with him. So he kept the small things of Dickie's that no one would remember—except maybe Marge—like the new blue address book that only had a few addresses in. She had probably given it to him. He also kept the rings, putting them in a little brown box where he stored other interesting bits and pieces he had collected over the years.

He sailed back to Naples the next day and immediately sent Dickie's two suitcases and some of his own "Dickie" paintings to the American Express in Venice, using the name "Robert Fanshaw" for the sender. He then took a train through Rome, Florence, Bologna, and Verona, where he got out and went by bus to the town of Trento about 40 miles away. There, he bought an old cream-colored car. He also bought a newspaper, but could find nothing about the search for Thomas Ripley, Freddie Miles, or the boat that was found in San Remo.

He slept in the car for a night. It was cold and awful, and he woke each time with pain in his neck and back. But that made his story more real, he thought. Next, he drove to Venice and found it bigger than he had expected, and full of more Italians than tourists. He liked being able to walk across the whole city, along the narrow streets and bridges, without getting into one of the narrow **gondolas**. He chose a hotel called the Costanza very near the Rialto bridge. It was clean and cheap—the right hotel for Tom Ripley—although he had almost more money with him than he could carry. He had cashed $1,000 of Dickie's traveler's checks before he left Palermo.

He bought more newspapers the next afternoon and went to read them in a restaurant in a tiny street near the Piazza San Marco. And there it was, on the second page:

POLICE SEARCH FOR MISSING AMERICAN

Dickie Greenleaf, Friend of the Murdered Freddie Miles,
Missing After Sicilian Holiday

Tom read it carefully. Dickie Greenleaf had been asked to come to Rome for questioning over the disappearance of his close friend Tom Ripley after a holiday in Sicily. Ripley had been missing for about three months, the paper said. The paper also mentioned the checks, saying that both Richard's Italian and American banks believed them to be forged. This was despite a letter from Richard Greenleaf that said they were his own. "Can anybody make a **forgery** against himself?" asked the paper. "Or is the wealthy American helping one of his friends?"

Tom put the paper down and acted shocked. He even ignored the waiter who was trying to give him the menu, until he touched his arm. He ate his lunch slowly and with pleasure, smoking a couple of cigarettes. Then, he got up and asked a policeman the way to the nearest police station. He was not afraid, but telling them he was Tom Ripley was one of the saddest things he had ever done in his life.

———————

The Venice police immediately called Rome and told them who had arrived and where he was staying. Then, they told him that someone who worked with the Rome police would come that evening after eight o'clock to find him. Tom spent the afternoon in his room making his hair darker. He put on his old glasses and wore his cheapest and oldest clothes—he wanted to look as different from Dickie as it was possible.

At eight thirty that evening, he was visited by the policeman Roverini, who had met him as Dickie in the apartment in Rome. His kind, smiling face did not look at all surprised or **suspicious**. Another, younger officer followed him into the room, and Tom realized nervously that this man had been with Roverini on the second of his visits.

Roverini sat down in the armchair that Tom offered him. He made the room dark, with only one small lamp switched on. It was the way he wanted it. "You are a friend of *Signor* Greenleaf?" Roverini asked.

"Yes." Tom sat down in another armchair in the darkest part of the room.

"When did you last see him, and where?" asked Roverini.

"I saw him for a short time in Rome, just before he went to Sicily."

"And, when you were in Rome, did he tell you the police were looking for you?" Roverini was writing it all down.

"No. I didn't know that *I* was missing." Tom smiled.

"Mr. Greenleaf should have told you," the policeman said, smiling. "He has not been very helpful. And where have you been since the end of November?"

"I've been traveling in the north—Milano, Torino, Pisa. I was sleeping in my car most of the time." Tom made lots of mistakes with his Italian, and his tone was rough and uneducated. He knew that he sounded very different from the Dickie that they had met in Rome.

"So this explains the mystery of the San Remo boat," said Roverini with a smile.

"What's that?" replied Tom, frowning.

"A boat was found in the water in San Remo. There was blood in it. You disappeared the same day that it went missing so we thought that something had happened to you. But you're alive."

"But didn't *Signor* Greenleaf tell you that I went to Mongibello after San Remo?" asked Tom, surprised. "I did some jobs for him."

"He did not." The policeman touched his thick mustache. "And did you know Frederick Miles?"

Tom shook his head. "No. I only met him once, in Naples. I never saw him again but . . . well, I'm not sure, but I think he was also in love with Marge—Dickie's girlfriend."

The policeman's eyes grew wide at that. "So you think maybe they argued about Miss Sherwood?"

"I can't say. It's possible. I read that you think Dickie killed Freddie. Is it true?"

"No, no, no!" the policeman cried. "But it is important that he shows himself in a police station. He was seen very drunk with Freddie Miles the night he died. But maybe Freddie wasn't drunk, but already dead. And why is *Signor* Greenleaf hiding from us?"

"I don't know," replied Tom. "As you say, he is not very helpful. He didn't tell me in Rome that the police were looking for me. But, at the same time, I can't believe that he killed Freddie Miles."

———

After they had left, Tom could have flown like a bird out the window. He felt so light and free. Those stupid policemen! They could not see any of it—never guessing that Dickie was dead and could never have killed Freddie Miles. And now he, Tom Ripley, was safe! He decided to have an expensive three-course dinner that night, somewhere he could stare at the beautiful Grand Canal.

He had an idea while he was getting ready. He was going to find an envelope and write on it that it should not be opened for several months to come. Inside it would be a **will** signed by Dickie, written on his old typewriter. The will would leave Tom all his money and his income. Now that was a good idea!

CHAPTER TWELVE

The palazzo

Venice
February 28th

Dear Mr. Greenleaf,

I hope you don't mind me writing to you about your son— but it seems that I was one of the last people who saw him. That was in Rome on February 2nd at the Inghilterra Hotel. As you know, this was only two or three days after the death of Freddie Miles. Dickie was upset and nervous. He said that he was going to Palermo as soon as the police finished questioning him. I felt he seemed very unhappy and that he might try to do something violent. He also said that he didn't want to see his friend Marge Sherwood again.

What I am trying to say is that I feel Richard may have killed himself, because he has not been found. This is a very sad message to send to you, but I am feeling more and more uncomfortable about this idea, and thought I should let you know.

Tom

———————

Mongibello
March 3rd

Dear Tom,

Thanks for your letter. I am going to Rome tomorrow to meet

Dickie's father, who is flying over. I just wanted to say that I don't agree at all that Dickie may have killed himself. Dickie just wasn't like that. I believe he might have been murdered in Naples, or he's hiding somewhere because he just doesn't want to see people.

But I'm glad you don't think the checks were forged. Dickie has changed so much since November, he could easily have changed his handwriting, too.

Nice to know your address finally. Thanks for your letter, your advice, and the invitations to Venice.

Marge

PS I didn't tell you my good news. I have a publisher interested in my Mongibello book. Now I just have to finish it!

She had decided she wanted to be friends with him despite the things she had said in her letter to Dickie about him, Tom supposed.

Dickie's disappearance was creating a lot of excitement in the Italian newspapers. There were photographs that Marge must have given them—of Dickie sitting on the beach alone in Mongibello and some of him with Marge. The newspapers called her "the girlfriend of both Richard Greenleaf and Freddie Miles." Tom was happy to be described as "a good friend" of Mr. Greenleaf, who had helped the police a lot. "Mr. Ripley," they went on to write, "a wealthy American, now lives in a *palazzo* next to the Piazza San Marco in Venice."

Tom had not thought of his place as a "palace" before. He had rented a beautiful old two-story house with an entrance on the Grand Canal that could only be approached by gondola. There was a very large key for this door, and another, smaller one for the normal "back" door, which led off the street. Tom had filled the insides with beautiful old furniture and expensive pictures. He had employed a maid—Anna—and her husband, Ugo, to clean and cook for him.

Because of the newspapers, Tom was well known in Venice now and had his choice of cocktail parties. He had made wealthy new friends, including a nice English man called Peter Smith-Kingsley and a real **countess**—the very sophisticated Countess (Titi) della Latta-Cacciaguerra. Everyone knew the name Tom Ripley and that he had been friends with Dickie Greenleaf. They all wanted to know him. Tom was always quiet and shy—he wanted to be seen as a gentle young man who was not used to being around lots of important people. The main emotion he showed them was worry about what had happened to Dickie.

On April 4th, he got a telephone call from Marge. She was at the train station in Venice.

"I'll come and pick you up," Tom said, happily. "Is Dickie's father with you?"

"No, he's in Rome. I'm alone. You don't have to pick me up. I've only got one bag, and I know where you live—it's next to della Salute, isn't it?"

"Well, OK. Have you had lunch?"

"No."

"Good."

He asked Anna to make lunch for two, and told her she and Ugo could have the afternoon off. Then, he made some cocktails. When he heard Marge knock on the door, he went and opened it.

"Marge! Good to see you! Come in!" He took the bag from her hand.

"How are you, Tom?" she said. "Wow, is this all yours?" She looked around her with wide eyes.

"I rented it very cheaply," Tom said. "Come and have a drink. Tell me what's new. You've been talking to the police in Rome—and Mr. Greenleaf?"

"Yes, and he's very upset, understandably," Marge said, sitting down on a sofa. "He's talking to all Dickie's friends, and to the police. He keeps saying that they would do a much better job in America. But they've found out that Dickie cashed over a thousand dollars of traveler's checks before he left Palermo. So, he must have gone off somewhere with it, like Greece or Africa. He wouldn't have killed himself after doing that."

"No," Tom agreed. He started asking her lots of questions, like what she had heard about the murder of Freddie Miles. She said that the doorman of Dickie's apartment had told the police that Freddie looked angry, like they had argued. Freddie had asked him if Dickie was living alone. Tom could tell that Marge was not suspicious about it at all.

At that moment, Anna came in and announced lunch. Tom noticed her eyes go wide as she saw Marge. She recognized her from the newspapers.

"So, what happened?" said Marge after Anna had left. She was looking around at the apartment again. "Did your aunt die and leave you all her money?"

"No, I just made a decision that I was going to enjoy what I have while it lasts," Tom replied, happily. "I had two thousand dollars left so I decided to spend it well and have a good time. The money should last until the summer. I feel I deserve it anyway, because I spent most of the winter traveling around and sleeping in a car. I know that you thought I was with Dickie, but I saw about as much of him as you did."

He made them two more cocktails. He could see she was a bit drunk now. During lunch, she asked him lots of questions about Dickie. Then, she said, "And how do you think he felt about me? Tell me honestly. I can take it."

"I think he was worried about you," Tom said, carefully. "It was the usual thing. He was terrified of marriage – "

"But I never asked him to marry me!" Marge cried.

"I know, but . . ." Tom did not want to say it, but he made himself continue. "I just don't think he liked the **responsibility** of you caring so much about him. I don't think he wanted a serious **relationship** with you." That told her everything and nothing.

Marge stared at him for a moment. Then, she sat up and said, "Well, that's all water under the bridge now.

I just want to know where Dickie has gone. I—Oh, I'm terribly sorry, Tom!" At that moment, she knocked over her cocktail, sending it all over the table. Tom ran to the kitchen.

"It's fine," he said, wiping the cocktail up. But he suddenly hated her. He remembered seeing her under clothes hanging over a chair on her terrace in Mongibello. They would be hanging over his chairs tonight if he invited her to stay here. But he looked up and gave her a huge smile. "I hope that you'll want to stay here tonight. I have two rooms upstairs, and you're welcome to one of them."

She smiled back at him. "Thanks a lot. All right. I will."

CHAPTER THIRTEEN
The rings

The next day, Tom received a telegram from Mr. Greenleaf.

HAVE DECIDED TO COME TO VENICE. WOULD LIKE TO
SEE YOU. ARRIVING 11:45 A.M.

Tom's body went cold. Well, he had expected it. But he
had not really. He hated the thought of it.

He and Marge went to meet Mr. Greenleaf at the train
station. It was raining again, and windy. Mr. Greenleaf
came through the gate looking pale and tired. Marge kissed
him on the cheek, and he smiled at her.

"Hello, Tom," he said in a friendly voice, and shook his
hand. "How are you?"

"Very well, sir. And you?"

They took Mr. Greenleaf to his hotel and then found a
restaurant to eat a seafood lunch.

"So, is there any news?" Marge asked as they sat down.

Mr. Greenleaf shook his head and looked nervously out
the window. He told them that the police had not found
out anything new, and he had arranged for an American
private detective to fly over. He did not think much of the
Italian police. Tom listened, thoughtfully. He, too, had a
suspicion that American detectives were better than Italian
ones.

"That's a good idea," he said. "Although I think the
Italian police are good. Does your detective speak Italian?"

"I really don't know," replied Mr. Greenleaf in a way that said he knew that he should have thought about that. "His name is McCarron. He's said to be very good. He's arriving tomorrow or the next day. I'm going back in the morning to meet him."

"Tom has the most beautiful house!" Marge said, suddenly. Tom turned toward her and tried to change his angry stare into a smile. The questions, he knew, would come at the house, when he and Mr. Greenleaf were alone.

But, when they got back to the house, Marge sat with them for another half an hour in Tom's sitting room. She kept saying how sure she was that Dickie was still alive. Then, finally, she got up and told them she was going upstairs to sleep. After she left, Mr. Greenleaf stood up and began to walk up and down with his hands in his pockets.

"Well, Tom," he said in a strange voice. "This is a strange end, isn't it?"

"End?"

"Well, you living in Europe now, and Richard . . . Well, where do you think he might be?"

"Well, sir, he could be hiding somewhere in Italy, staying in small hotels and using a false name. Though I'm sorry to say it, Mr. Greenleaf, but I think it's very likely that Richard is dead."

Mr. Greenleaf's face did not change. "Because he was so unhappy in Rome? What did he say to you?"

Tom frowned. "I think the Freddie Miles murder had shaken him. He hated the newspapers being so interested

78

and said if one more thing happened he'd—well, that he didn't know what he would do. Also, for the first time I felt he wasn't interested in his painting."

Mr. Greenleaf looked up at the ceiling. "I wish that we could find this Di Massimo. He might know something. If he was real. The police can't find any painter called Di Massimo."

"I never knew him," Tom said. "But Dickie talked about him a couple of times. I'm sure he was real."

"You said, 'if one more thing happened to him.' What else happened to him?"

"Well, I didn't realize it then," Tom said, slowly, "but I think I know what Dickie meant now. The police had questioned him about the boat in San Remo. Did they tell you about that?"

Tom had practiced what he told Mr. Greenleaf next, because it was better that he heard it from Tom than the police. "They found a boat in San Remo under the water. It had blood on it. The boat disappeared on the same day Dickie and I were there, and we'd gone out in the same kind of boat. They found the boat just after the Miles murder, and they couldn't find me at the time because I was traveling around the country. So they asked Dickie where I was. I think that for a while they suspected Dickie of killing me!"

"Good God!"

"I only know this because a policeman told me. I didn't know that I was being looked for until I read about it in a newspaper. Of course, now they know I'm still alive. But the reason I'm mentioning it is that Dickie knew the police were looking for me, but he never told me when I was in Rome. He didn't want to help them. He seemed to want to let the police find me. He wasn't going to tell them where I was."

Mr. Greenleaf shook his head in a fatherly way that said he could believe it of Dickie.

"I think that was the night he said that if one more thing happened to him . . ." Tom finished.

"I'm sorry, but I just don't believe that Richard killed himself," said Mr. Greenleaf.

"Well, neither does Marge," replied Tom, slowly. "I just think it's possible, that's all. Though I think it's more likely that he's hiding. He could have gone to Greece or France or anywhere after he got back to Naples, because no one was looking for him until days later."

"I know, I know," Mr. Greenleaf said, tiredly.

That evening, Tom and Marge met Mr. Greenleaf for dinner. He was happier now because he had just telephoned his wife, and she was feeling better. It was a quiet dinner with just two courses, which Mr. Greenleaf paid for. Then, he said he was going back to his hotel because he did not feel very well. Tom noticed that he was not eating much and wondered if he had found, like many other newly arrived tourists, that the Italian food did not agree with him. But you did not ask things like that to people like Mr. Greenleaf.

Marge decided that she would travel back to Rome with Dickie's father the next morning. They all walked back to his hotel and said goodnight, then Tom and Marge went for some drinks and coffee in a bar. It was very late when they took a gondola back to Tom's house—it was Marge who wanted it, of course. Tom had a bad taste in his mouth from the strong coffee, and his heart was beating hard. He *hated* gondolas. He felt tired and lay back in the boat while Marge talked happily. It seemed to take forever to reach the steps to his house, and as the gondola pulled away he suddenly realized he did not have the big key to the front door.

Before he could say something, Marge started laughing. "You didn't bring the key? Water on every side and no key!"

Tom tried to smile. Why would he have brought a heavy key that was nearly a foot long? He turned and shouted to the **gondolier** to come back. But the man kept on going.

Marge laughed again. "Oh, it doesn't matter. Another gondolier will come past soon. Isn't it beautiful here?"

But it was not a beautiful night. It was cold, and there were no gondolas anywhere. Finally, a small motorboat came by and took them to the nearest landing place.

When they got inside, Marge went upstairs to pack her things and go to bed, and Tom sat down to read a letter he had received that afternoon from Bob Delancey. It was the first time he had heard from Bob since he got to Italy except for one postcard. Bob said that the police had visited the house and were questioning everyone about a tax **fraud**. The **defrauder** had used the address of Bob's house to receive his checks and had called himself George McAlpin. Bob seemed to think it was rather funny. The defrauder had not even tried to cash the checks, so it was not much of a fraud, Bob explained.

Tom thought about New York and the strange life that people lived there. How boring it seemed compared to wonderful Italy. "I am jealous of you, living there in Venice!" Bob wrote. "Do you take lots of gondola rides? What are the girls there like? How long are you staying anyway?"

"Forever," Tom thought, closing his eyes. Maybe he would never go back to America. It was the evenings in Italy he loved the most. Either spent here or in Rome alone, wearing his clothes or Dickie's, and staring at his things and the beautiful place that he lived.

"Tom?" He opened his eyes. Marge was coming down the stairs barefoot. She had his small brown box in her hand. "I've just found Dickie's rings," she said.

CHAPTER FOURTEEN

More questions

Tom stood up. "Oh, he gave them to me to look after," he said, quickly.

"When?"

"In Rome, I think, before he went to Palermo." He took a step back and pulled off one of his shoes then picked it up in both hands.

"What was he going to do?" Marge said, with wide eyes. "Why did he give them to you?"

He wondered why she had looked in the box but did not ask her. "He said, if anything ever happened to him, he wanted me to have his rings." He was holding the shoe in both hands now. How he would do it went quickly through his head. He would hit her on the head with the heavy wooden bottom part of the shoe, then pull her out and throw her body into the canal. He would tell everyone that she had fallen on the wet steps there and hit her head.

She looked down at the box. "Then, Dickie *was* going to kill himself."

He was silent for a moment, realizing her meaning. "Yes," he said, "I suppose if you look at it that way—the rings—they make it more likely."

"Why didn't you say anything about it before?"

"I think I forgot about them. I put them away so they wouldn't get lost, and I never thought of looking at them again."

"You had better tell Mr. Greenleaf—and the police."

Tom looked at her. She was about to cry. This was the first moment that she had allowed herself to think that Dickie was probably dead, he realized. He dropped the shoe, put his foot back into it, and went to put his arms round her. He could smell her perfume—the Stradivari probably. "Maybe he did kill himself then," he said.

"Yes," she said, into his shoulder. Then, she turned suddenly, her eyes filled with tears, and went quickly back up the stairs. She was too upset to speak.

He sat down on the sofa. He felt as tired as he had after he had killed Freddie Miles, or after Dickie in San Remo. He had been so close to killing her! He remembered his cool thoughts of throwing her in the canal and thought of the words he would say to Mr. Greenleaf. He heard his own voice saying, "I stood there on the steps calling to her, but I wasn't sure she'd hurt herself. I thought it was a joke." And inside he would be calm because his story was good—*so good* that he would come to believe it himself. But what frightened him was that he had already done it twice before. He could tell himself that he had not wanted to murder them, but he *had* murdered them. Of course, he felt regret. What was happening to him? What *had* happened? He had to face Mr. Greenleaf with the rings tomorrow. He would have to tell him the same story that he had told Marge. He started to think about it again, adding more information. He imagined Dickie taking off his rings and giving them to him, and his voice saying, "Listen, Tom, don't tell anyone about this."

———

Marge rang Mr. Greenleaf at eight thirty the next morning. They arranged to meet him in his hotel room at nine thirty and traveled there by gondola. It was another cold, wet day. Mr. Greenleaf opened the door for them, and Tom saw a short, fat man of about 35 standing by the window. He must be the private detective. "This is Alvin McCarron," Mr. Greenleaf said. "He's come straight from the airport. This is Miss Sherwood and Tom Ripley."

Tom felt McCarron looking at him. "So you're a friend of Richard's?" he asked.

"We both are," said Tom. They all sat down round a table at the far side of the room. Marge took the rings from her purse and gave them to McCarron. Then, Tom repeated the same story he had told Marge the night before. The detective listened carefully with a face that was hard to read. McCarron asked about the time and date he had given the rings to him, and if Dickie had been drunk.

"No. He drinks very little," Tom replied. "He told me not to mention the rings to anyone, and of course I agreed. I put them in an old box that I have and forgot about them."

The detective looked at him silently for a moment and Tom waited, his body ready for a difficult question, or even an **accusation**.

"And is he the kind of man to lend you the rings for a

short time?" McCarron said.

"No," Marge said, before Tom could answer. "I can't imagine Dickie without his rings."

"And what do you think, Mr. Ripley?" the detective said, staring at him.

"I'm afraid I agree with Miss Sherwood that it looks as if he's killed himself," Tom replied.

The detective then went on to ask him and Marge questions. When had they both last seen Dickie? What about the murder of Freddie Miles? He asked about the checks, but both Tom and Marge told him that they did not believe Dickie had forged them. Then, McCarron stood up and said to Tom, "Would you mind coming downstairs with me, if you have a few minutes?"

Tom followed him downstairs and into the reception area. "Is this the way they do it?" he thought. "A quiet word and then an accusation. Then after that he'll give me over to the Italian police?"

"Shall we go in here?" McCarron said, and led him into the coffee bar. "I wanted to talk to you about Richard alone," he said. "What kind of man is he?"

Was McCarron going to approach his arrest like this? Or did he want an opinion on Dickie that Dickie's father and girlfriend could not give him?

"He wanted to be a painter," Tom replied. "But he wasn't very good. He acted like he didn't care, but I think Italian life was making him unhappy. And things were difficult with Marge."

"How do you mean?"

"She was in love with him, and he wasn't in love with her. He was never going to marry her, but Marge wouldn't give up. I think that's why Dickie left Mongibello. He told me this in Rome when I saw him. He seemed nervous and said that, after the Miles murder, he didn't want to see Marge. He was worried she would come to Rome when she heard about it."

McCarron drank some of his coffee. "Why do you think he was nervous after the Miles murder?"

Because they had been good friends, Tom explained, and Freddie had been killed just a few minutes after leaving his house.

"Do you think Richard killed Freddie?"

"No, I don't. He had no reason."

"Do you think that Richard was the kind of man who could kill someone?"

Tom frowned for a moment, like someone trying hard to discover the truth.

"I never thought about it," he said, finally. "I don't know what kind of people are likely to kill someone. But I've seen him angry."

"When?"

Tom talked about the two days in Rome when Dickie had moved out of his apartment to avoid phone calls from friends and strangers. At the same time, he had grown more and more unhappy about his painting. He described Dickie as a proud young man who was angry with his father and did not want to work in the family business. His moods changed very quickly, Tom explained, being nice to strangers and then suddenly angry with friends for no reason.

"It would explain a lot if he had killed Freddie Miles, wouldn't it?"

"Yes," Tom said. "Everything."

"Well, this is only my first day of work," McCarron said with a smile. "I haven't looked at the police report in Rome. I'll probably want to talk to you again after I've been there."

Tom stared at him. It seemed to be over. "Are you going to Rome today?" he asked.

"Yes, in a couple of hours—with Mr. Greenleaf."

"Do you speak Italian?"

"Not very well, but I can read it. My French is better," McCarron said, as if it were not important.

It was *very* important, Tom thought. He could not imagine McCarron getting all the information he needed from Roverini, neither would he be able to talk to the doorman at the apartment in Rome.

McCarron finished his coffee and stood up. "Knowing Dickie, what places do you think he might go if he wanted to hide?" he asked.

"Well, I know he likes Italy best. He also likes Greece, and all of Spain is a possibility, I suppose."

"I see," McCarron said, suddenly looking tired. "Well, thank you, Mr. Ripley. I have your address and phone number if I need to speak to you again."

CHAPTER FIFTEEN

The will

Mr. Greenleaf, McCarron, and Marge all left for Rome together. Tom spent the afternoon at home expecting a telephone call from the detective but none came. There was only a call from Countess Titi inviting him to a cocktail party that evening.

The following day, McCarron called, but he only wanted to know all the names of Dickie's friends in Mongibello and Naples. Tom went through them all with their difficult addresses—all except *Signor* Pucci, who had sold the house and boat for him.

"You never met this painter, Di Massimo?" McCarron asked.

"No. I saw him once," Tom said. "But I never met him."

"What did he look like?"

"Well, it was just on a street corner. I left Dickie as he was going to meet him, so I wasn't very close to him. He looked about five feet nine, about fifty, gray-black hair. He wore a light-gray suit."

"Um, OK," McCarron said, slowly, as if he were writing all that down. "Well, that's about everything. Thanks very much, Mr. Ripley."

"You're welcome. Good luck."

The weeks went past, and there were no more calls. Tom went to more parties and spent time with his wealthy friends. Peter Smith-Kingsley had a couple of English newspapers that his friends had sent him. There were pictures in them of Tom in the streets of Venice, and one of his house.

"I'm so tired of it," Tom said. "I'm only staying here to try to help if I can, but there are journalists everywhere."

"I understand," Peter said. "I'm going home at the end of May, you know. If you'd like to come along and stay at my place in Ireland, you'd be welcome. It's very quiet there."

Tom stared at him. Peter had told him about his old Irish castle and had shown him pictures of it. Then, Tom had a sudden memory of his relationship with Dickie, like a pale ghost. The same thing could happen with Peter, he realized. Peter, who was kind and not at all suspicious, except that he—Tom—did not look enough like Peter. But one night he had spoken in an English-sounding voice and acted like Peter, and Peter had thought it was really funny. It now made Tom feel terribly ashamed.

"Thanks," he said, and suddenly he was nearly crying, "but I'd better stay by myself for a little longer. I miss my friend Dickie, you know. I miss him terribly."

"Don't worry," replied Peter, softly, touching him on the shoulder. "Of course you do. I'd really think something was wrong with you if you didn't feel like this."

———————

Venice
June 3rd

Dear Mr. Greenleaf,
    While I was packing today, I found an envelope that Richard gave me in Rome, and that I'd completely forgotten about. On the envelope was written "Not to be opened until June" and, of course, now it is June. Inside it I found a will written by Richard that leaves everything to me. I am very shocked by this, as I'm sure you are, too.
    I am so sorry that I did not remember having the envelope because it would have shown much earlier that Richard planned to take his own life. I put it in a suitcase pocket and then forgot about it. I am sending a copy of the will so that you may see it for yourself. This is the first will I have ever seen in my life, and I don't know what to do next.
    Please say hello to Mrs. Greenleaf for me and tell her how sorry I am that I had to write this letter. It would be good to hear from you as soon as possible. My next address will be:

c/o American Express, Athens, Greece

Yours,
    Tom Ripley

It was asking for trouble, but he only had $2,000 left in his bank, and he knew he must not take any more from Dickie's account, so why not try for all his money?! He had bought his ticket for the voyage to Greece in the middle of May, and the days had grown warmer. He was so bored after the gray, quiet weeks in Venice. He guessed that he was safe—he had not heard from Roverini, and even the newspapers had stopped writing about Dickie and Freddie Miles.

Two days before Tom sailed, he went to tea at the house of Countess Titi della Latta-Cacciaguerra. The maid showed him into the living room, and Titi entered soon after. "Ah, Tomaso!" she cried, her arms wide with excitement. "Have you seen the afternoon newspaper? They have found Dickie's suitcases! Right here in the American Express in Venice!"

"What?" Tom had not seen the papers.

"Read it! Here! They were sent from Naples. Perhaps he is here in Venice!"

Tom read the story carefully. The paper around Dickie's paintings had come undone, and someone had noticed Dickie's "signature" on them. The police were now looking at everything for **fingerprints**.

"Perhaps he is alive!" shouted Titi.

"I don't think this means he is alive," said Tom. "It says here that the suitcases and paintings were sent under the name Robert Fanshaw. Dickie could have been murdered, or killed himself after he sent the suitcases. His passport was even there. He packed his passport."

"Perhaps he is hiding himself under the name of Robert Fanshaw! Oh, sit down, Tom, you need some tea!"

"But it says here that he packed all his bathroom stuff—and his shoes and coat. Everything. He couldn't be alive and leave all that. The murderer must have taken his clothes and put everything in the American Express. It was probably the easiest way to get rid of it."

He was not leaving until the day after tomorrow, Tom thought. There was lots of time for Roverini to get his—Tom's—fingerprints and compare them to the stuff in the suitcases, and then to Dickie's. Wouldn't Mr. Greenleaf have sent Dickie's fingerprints from America immediately?

He tried to turn his thoughts to Greece. To him, Greece was a place covered in gold. He imagined stone statues with strong, calm faces. He did not want to go to Greece with questions about fingerprints and the police hanging over his head. It would make him feel so ashamed, as low as it was possible to feel. Tom dropped his face in his hands and began to cry.

Titi put her fat arm round him. "Tomaso, why are you crying? Wait until you have a reason to be unhappy."

"I can't see why you don't see that this is a bad sign!" Tom said, sadly. "I really don't!"

By the time he got on the ship to Athens, Tom was like a walking ghost. He had heard nothing from Roverini, and that was a bad sign as his messages before had always been so friendly. He stayed in his cabin most of the time and had not been able to sleep or eat for days. He knew that Mr.

Greenleaf had received the letter about the will now. If the police discovered his fingerprints on Dickie's things, and then that the signature on the will was also forged, it might put Tom in the electric chair.

He spent that evening walking up and down the ship and talking to no one. He just wanted to be alone. What if the captain was just now receiving a message to arrest Tom Ripley? He, Tom, would stand up bravely, or he might throw himself into the sea. Well, what if he did? He was not afraid. If they got him on the fingerprints and on the will, had it been worth the months from November until now? Of course it had.

He wished that he had seen more of the world, that was all. He wanted to see Australia and India. He wanted to see Japan. Since knowing Dickie, he had become interested in paintings. He did not want to be a painter, but, if he had the money, he wanted to collect them.

The following morning, the boat approached Greece. Tom stood at the front and saw four policemen standing in a line with folded arms, staring up at the ship. Tom collected his suitcases and walked down on to the harbor, then turned toward the policemen. "I'll just tell them who I am," he thought. "I won't shout or run."

The policemen stared back at him. He smiled at them a little. Then, one of them touched his hat, and they all stood to one side. He walked between them toward a newspaper shop, and they did not look at him at all.

CHAPTER SIXTEEN

In Greece

Tom stared at the different newspapers in front of him, feeling strange and lightheaded. He pulled out one French and one Italian newspaper and paid for them with lire. The policemen were still not looking at him. He read the papers while he was waiting for a bus to Athens.

NO ONE NAMED ROBERT FANSHAW FOUND

said one on the second page. Only the fifth paragraph of the article interested Tom.

> The police decided a few days ago that fingerprints on the suitcases and paintings are the same as the fingerprints found in Mr. Greenleaf's apartment in Rome. They have decided that they are definitely Mr. Greenleaf's fingerprints.

And on the page of the other paper . . .

> The police have decided that *Signor* Greenleaf sent the suitcases to Venice himself, and then killed himself. Or he may still be living under the name of Fanshaw. The police believe it is time to give up searching for Richard Greenleaf as he is not traveling under his "Richard Greenleaf" passport.

Tom got on the bus for Athens. There would be a letter about the will waiting for him at the American Express in Athens, Tom was sure. Perhaps the letter would be a polite "no" from Mr. Greenleaf's lawyer followed by a letter from the police saying that he was wanted for forgery. The will could undo it all. Maybe the Greek police would be waiting for him at the American Express.

The bus stopped in the city. Tom got out and found a taxi. "Would you take me to the American Express, please?" he said in Italian, but thankfully the man seemed to understand him.

When they arrived, he sat up straight and looked around the building for policemen. Perhaps they were inside. He asked the driver to wait, and he seemed to understand that, too. Everything felt very easy and calm.

He walked up to the desk. "Have you got any letters for Thomas Ripley?" he asked, quietly, in English.

The young woman turned and searched, then smiled. "Two letters," she said.

One was from Titi in Venice. The other was from Mr. Greenleaf.

June 9th

Dear Tom,

I received your letter of June 3rd yesterday.

The will was not such a surprise to me and my wife—we both knew that Richard cared a lot about you, even if he didn't say this in his letters. As you say, this does seem to suggest that Richard took his own life. It is also possible that Richard has taken another name and decided to turn his back on his family.

My wife agrees with me that we should do what Richard wanted, so I have given the copy of the will to my lawyers, who will take things forward from here.

Thank you again for your help when I was in Italy. Please write to us.

With best wishes,
    Herbert Greenleaf

Was it a joke? But of course Mr. Greenleaf would not joke about this. Tom walked out to the waiting taxi. It was no joke. It was his! Dickie's money and his life—his wonderful, free life. He could have a house in Europe and a house in America, too, if he chose.

After Athens, he was going to go to Crete. He imagined the tall mountains, the young men waiting for his cases, and the money he would give them for carrying them. He would have plenty of it to give them! Then, his body suddenly went cold as he imagined the line of Cretan policemen waiting for him on the harbor wall. Would he imagine policemen waiting for him at every harbor that he sailed to? In Alexandria? Istanbul? Bombay? Rio? But it was stupid to think about that. He pulled his shoulders back.

"To a hotel, please," Tom said to the taxi driver. "The best one, the best!"

During-reading questions

CHAPTERS ONE AND TWO

1 Why is Tom worried about the man who follows him into the bar?
2 What does Mr. Greenleaf want Tom to do? Why?
3 How does Dickie feel when he first meets Tom, do you think?

CHAPTERS THREE AND FOUR

1 How does Tom manage to change the way that Dickie feels about him?
2 Why is Marge angry with Dickie and Tom?
3 In Chapter Four, Dickie's feelings about Tom change again. Why?

CHAPTERS FIVE AND SIX

1 How does Tom feel when Dickie tells him he wants to go to Cortina with Marge. Why does he feel like this?
2 "He was pushing Tom out into the cold." What does Tom mean when he thinks this?
3 How does Tom hide Dickie's body?

CHAPTERS SEVEN AND EIGHT

1 What does "Dickie" tell Marge about their relationship in his letter?
2 How does Tom "practice" behaving like Dickie?
3 Why does Freddie think Tom is living with Dickie?
4 Why does Freddie come back to the apartment?

CHAPTERS NINE AND TEN

1 What does Tom want the police to believe about Freddie's murder?
2 What second piece of news in the newspapers shocks Tom?
3 Why does the dream frighten Tom?
4 What does Marge think about Dickie now?
5 What makes Tom's blood turn cold?

CHAPTERS ELEVEN AND TWELVE

1 What plan does Tom make to become himself again?
2 What plan does Tom make next?
3 How does Tom explain how he is now living in the palazzo to Marge?

CHAPTERS THIRTEEN AND FOURTEEN

1 What is a "private detective," do you think?
2 What does Bob tell Tom in his letter? Who is the real defrauder?
3 After Marge finds the rings, what does she think has happened to Dickie?
4 Read McCarron's questions to Tom, and Tom's answers, on pages 86–88. What does Tom make the private detective think about Dickie?

CHAPTERS FIFTEEN AND SIXTEEN

1 What reason does Tom give Peter for wanting to stay in Venice?
2 What do the police find in Venice?
3 Why does Tom's body go "cold" at the end of the story? What does this tell us about his future, do you think?

After-reading questions

1 "That was whether Dickie loved her or not, and Tom was sure that he did not." Do you agree with Tom that Dickie did not love Marge? Was Tom jealous of Marge, do you think?

2 Is Tom completely bad, do you think, or do you sometimes feel sorry for him?

3 Why doesn't Dickie want to go back to America, do you think?

4 Did Tom want to murder Dickie? If your answer is no, then what did Tom really want, do you think?

Exercises

CHAPTERS ONE AND TWO

1 **Write the correct word in your notebook.**

1 noimce ....*income*......... money that a person gets from working or because they come from a rich family

2 uhomr .... being funny, or the ability to know when things are funny

3 niluts .... when you do or say something rude or unkind to someone

4 oygvea .... a long journey on a boat or ship

5 rdwno .... to die underwater because you cannot breathe

6 hccke .... a small piece of paper from your bank that you write on and sign and use to pay for things

7 omdo .... how a person feels

8 ugstseg .... to offer an idea for someone to consider

2 **Write the correct verb form,** *present perfect* **or** *past*
perfect, **in your notebook.**

1 "So, what *.have.* you been doing? I thought you *'d/had.* gone."

2 Tom could see that Dickie was a bit worried, but not enough
to talk to her about it because he .... not seen her alone since
Tom moved in.

3 That kiss — it .... not looked like a first kiss.

4 "Why?" he said. "Why should she? What .... I ever done?"

5 No one .... ever said it directly to him before. Not in
this way.

6 When a couple of the men .... tried to kiss him, he had
rejected them.

7 "I care about her, and she's been very nice to me. We've ....
some good times together."

8 By five o'clock, after he .... finished painting, everything
would be forgotten.

3 **What happens here? Match in your notebook.**

Example: 4—e

1	Dickie's studio	a	Tom and Dickie watch some acrobats make a human tower.
2	Cannes	b	Tom decides to kill Dickie.
3	The train	c	Tom tells Marge that Dickie has moved to Rome.
4	The motorboat	d	Tom talks to Dickie about going to Paris in a coffin.
5	Mongibello	e	Tom kills Dickie with an oar.

4 **Complete these sentences with the correct word in your notebook.**

| typewriter | arrogance | checks | signature |
| publisher | make-up | forging | folding |

1 When he got to his room, he took out Dickie's old
...*typewriter*.... and wrote Marge a letter.

2 Tom bought some .... to put on his face.

3 He spent the evening practicing .... Dickie's .... for the bank ....

4 An American .... was interested in Marge's book.

5 Tom continued packing, ... Dickie's shirts lovingly into the suitcases.

6 He could feel the .... and anger building in Freddie and was a little afraid of him.

5 **Write questions for these answers in your notebook.**

1 *What did Tom find in Freddie's pocket?*..
He found a wallet and some keys.

2 He wanted the police to think that Freddie had been drunk.

3 He dreamed that Dickie was still alive.

4 He went to Sicily.

5 Because he wanted Mr. and Mrs. Greenleaf to believe that Dickie was still alive.

6 Because they suspected the signature on Dickie's check had been forged.

6 **Who is thinking this, do you think? Write the correct name in your notebook.**

> Tom   Marge   Anna   Marge
> Tom's friends in Venice   Mr. Greenleaf   Tom

1 I really enjoyed being Dickie Greenleaf. I don't want to be Tom again. .....*Tom*.....
2 I'm free! I'm free! They don't suspect me!
3 This man has a lovely house, and he's almost famous. We want to get to know him!
4 It is nice that Tom has written to us, but I don't agree that Dickie has killed himself.
5 I know that woman's face. I'm sure that I have seen her in the newspapers.
6 How did Tom get the money for this beautiful house?
7 I don't understand. I didn't want to marry Dickie.

7 **Use the adjectives to describe these people in your notebook. Can you think of any other adjectives?**

> worried   wealthy   careful   ashamed   jealous
> unwell   arrogant   clever   kind   suspicious
> attractive   lonely   friendly

1 Tom: .*arrogant*.
2 Marge: ....
3 Mr. Greenleaf: ....
4 Detective McCarron: ....

CHAPTERS FIFTEEN AND SIXTEEN

8 **Write the question tags in your notebook.**

1 Mr. Greenleaf, McCarron, and Marge all left together,
...*didn't they...* ?

2 Tom didn't want to go and stay with Peter in Ireland, ... ?

3 The police were now looking at everything for
fingerprints, ... ?

4 He had not heard anything from Roverini, ... ?

5 He wanted to see Australia and India, ... ?

6 But, of course, Mr. Greenleaf would not joke about
this, ... ?

7 Dickie's money was all his, ... ?

8 He would always imagine policemen waiting in a line
for him, ... ?

ALL CHAPTERS

9 **What do these sayings from the story mean? Write
your answers in your notebook.**

1 *speak very highly of you* Chapter One, page 6
to say good things about a person....

2 *heavy-handed* Chapter Two, page 18

3 *pulled on the Italian cigarette* Chapter Three, page 19

4 *Tom decided to give Dickie some space* Chapter Four, page 29

5 *so what?* Chapter Five, page 34

6 *has come up* Chapter Ten, page 61

7 *I can take it.* Chapter Twelve, page 75

8 *barefoot* Chapter Thirteen, page 82

9 *hanging over his head* Chapter Fifteen, page 93

10 *turn his back on* Chapter Sixteen, page 98

Project work

1 Imagine you are Marge. Write a day in your diary about your life with Dickie in Mongibello.
2 Write Chapter Six from *The Talented Mr. Ripley* as a play script.
3 Look online, and read about Venice. Make a presentation about it.
4 Compare the book to the film of *The Talented Mr. Ripley* (1999). How are they the same/different? Why did the writer make these changes for the film, do you think?
5 What happens to Tom after the story ends, do you think? Write reasons for your answers.
6 Write a newspaper report about Freddie's murder.

Essay questions

- What are the key events that lead up to Tom deciding to murder Dickie? (500 words)
- Do you think this story could happen, or would the police be more suspicious about Tom? (500 words)
- Tom is a nicer person than Dickie, he has just been unlucky in life. Do you agree? (500 words)
- In what ways does Tom make himself believe his own lies? (500 words)

An answer key for all questions and exercises can be found at **www.penguinreaders.co.uk**

Glossary

accusation (n.)
when you say that someone has done something wrong

acrobat (n.)
a person who can jump, balance and move their body in difficult ways. People enjoy watching *acrobats* at a circus, for example.

anchor (n.)
a heavy metal object that you drop into water from a boat to stop the boat from moving away

arrogant (adj.); **arrogance** (n.)
An *arrogant* person thinks that they are better or more important than other people. *Arrogance* is the noun of *arrogant*.

ashamed (adj.)
1) feeling worried about what other people might think of something bad or difficult in your life
2) feeling guilty because you have done something wrong

ashtray (n.)
a small, flat bowl for the ends of cigarettes or cigarette ash (= very small grey pieces that are left after something has burned)

atmosphere (n.)
the feeling created by a place or situation

cabin (n.)
a small bedroom on a ship

cancer (n.)
a serious illness that makes cells (= the smallest living parts of the body) grow in a way that is not normal. Many people die from *cancer*.

cash (n. and v.)
Cash is money as paper or coins. If you *cash* a *check*, you give the *check* to a bank and the bank gives you *cash* for it.

check (n.)
a small piece of paper from your bank that you write on and sign and use to pay for things

cocktail (n.)
a drink made by mixing two or more drinks together. *Cocktails* usually contain alcohol. A *cocktail* party is a party in the early evening where people have *cocktails* or other drinks and small things to eat.

coffin (n.)
a long box for a dead body

countess (n.)
in some countries in Europe, a title for a very *wealthy* woman from an important family

course (n.)
one of the parts of a meal. A
three-*course* dinner has three parts.

crook (n.)
a person who is not honest and
cheats people or steals things

disapproval (n.);
disapproving (adj.)
Disapproval is thinking that
something or someone is bad
or wrong. If you say or do
something in a *disapproving* way,
you say or do it in a way that
shows *disapproval*.

drown (v.)
to die under water because you
cannot breathe

drugs (n.)
something that people take to
make themselves feel happy,
excited, etc. Buying and selling
drugs is against the law.

easel (n.)
something you use to hold a
picture while you paint it. An
easel is usually made of wood.

emotion (n.)
a strong feeling like love, sadness
or anger

fingerprints (n.)
marks made by the end
of your finger when you
touch something. The police
sometimes use *fingerprints* to help
them discover who did a crime.

fold (v.); **folded** (adj.)
If you *fold* a piece of paper,
material, etc., you press one
part of it over another part. If
a person's arms are *folded,* they
have put one of their arms over
the other and are holding them
against their body.

forge (v.); **forgery** (n.)
If you *forge* a *signature, check,* etc.,
you make a copy of it because
you want to trick people by
making them think that the copy
is real. This is *forgery.* A *forgery* is
also the copy of something that is
made to trick people.

for God's sake (phr.)
You say *for God's sake* when you
want to show that something has
made you angry.

fraud (n.); **fraudster** (n.);
defrauder (n.);
Fraud is the crime of getting
money by doing things that are
not honest, often by cheating
people or using *forgery.* A *fraudster*
or *defrauder* is a person who
does this.

frown (v.)
to move the top part of your face
to show that you are not happy
or that you are thinking hard

gay (adj.)
A *gay* man has sex with other
men. A *gay* woman has sex with
other women.

get rid of (phr. v.)
to make something or someone
go away or take them to another
place because you do not
want them

gin and tonic (n.)
Gin is a strong, clear drink with
alcohol in it. *Tonic* is a soda drink
which has bubbles (= balls of
gas) in it and tastes a little bitter
(= not sweet). It is often added
to *gin*.

gondola (n.); **gondolier** (n.)
a long, narrow boat with high
parts at each end. *Gondolas* are
used in Venice. A *gondolier's* job is
to take people for rides around
Venice in *gondolas*.

graveyard (n.)
an area, often outside a church,
where dead people are put under
the ground

G-string (n.)
a narrow piece of material
which is worn to cover the parts
between a person's legs and is
held up by a very thin piece
of material

hint (n.)
something that you say or
do to show what you are
thinking, without saying it in
a direct way

humor (n.)
being funny, or the ability to
know when things are funny

income (n.)
money that a person gets from
working or because they come
from a rich family

influence (n. and v.)
when something or someone
affects what a person thinks or
does. If something or someone
is a bad *influence* on someone,
they make them behave badly.

insult (n. and v.)
when you do or say something
rude or unkind to someone.
If you feel *insulted*, you feel
that someone has said or done
something rude or unkind
to you.

Internal Revenue (n.)
In the United States, the
Department of *Internal Revenue*
is the part of the government that
is responsible for collecting taxes.
The collector of *Internal Revenue*
is a person whose job is to collect
taxes for the government.

lire (n.)
the money that was used in Italy
until the euro (€) was introduced
in 2002. We say *lira* for one
of them.

maid (n.)
a woman whose job is to clean,
cook or do other work in
someone's home

make up (phr. v.)
to become friends with someone
again after you have argued
with them

make-up (n.)
special colours that you put
on your face to make you look
different or more beautiful

missing (adj.)
If a person or thing is or goes
missing, you cannot find them.

mood (n.)
how a person feels. If a person is
in a good *mood*, they feel happy.
If they are in a bad *mood*, they
feel angry or sad.

motorboat (n.); **motor** (n.)
A *motor* is an engine that makes
a machine move or work. A
motorboat is a small boat with a
motor that makes it move.

oar (n.)
a long wooden stick that you
push and pull to make a boat
move through water

perfume (n.)
a liquid (= a thing like water) that
people put on their skin to make
them smell nice

publisher (n.)
someone who works with
authors to make and sell
their books

regret (n. and v.)
when you feel sad or sorry about
something that you have done or
did not do

relationship (n.)
1) a special friendship where
two people love each other and
have sex
2) the way people are when
they are together. If they like
each other, they have a good
relationship. If they do not like
each other, they have a bad
relationship.

responsibility (n.)
something that you should or
must do

second-rate (adj.)
not very good, or not as good
as others

signature (n.)
your name written by you in
your own way

sissy (n.)
an unkind word for a boy who
someone thinks is weak and only
interested in the kinds of things
that girls like

slam (v.)
If you *slam* a door, you close it
with a loud noise.

sophisticated (adj.)
having experience of the world
and knowing about fashion,
modern ideas, etc.

studio (n.)
a special room where an artist
paints or draws pictures

suggest (v.)
1) to offer an idea for someone
to consider
2) to show that something is likely
or true

suspect (v.); **suspicious** (adj.)
to *suspect* someone or something
is to believe that a person has
done something wrong or that
something bad has happened. If
you are *suspicious* about something,
you have a feeling that something
bad is true or will happen.

tear (n.)
a small amount of water that
comes out of your eyes when
you cry

telegram (n.)
in the past, a short, important
message that was sent using
electricity and printed on paper

terrace (n.)
a flat area outside a house or
restaurant where you can sit
or eat

tone (n.)
the way that a person's voice
sounds when they are angry,
happy, etc.

trust fund (n.)
money that is controlled for
someone by another person
or organization

turn up (phr. v.)
to happen or be there in a way
that was not expected or planned

typewriter (n.)
a machine with buttons that
you press to write letters and
numbers on paper. *Typewriters*
were used before computers.

voyage (n.)
a long journey on a boat or ship.
You say *Bon voyage* to a person
who is going to travel to tell
them that you hope they have
a good journey.

wallet (n.)
a small, flat case for money,
credit cards, etc. that you carry
in your pocket

wealthy (adj.)
rich

will (n.)
a document that gives
information about who will get
your money and other things
that you own after you die